For the Good
of the Order

Dyslexic Friendly Version

JERRY FRANCIS

Paper back ISBN-13: 978-1-963272-08-6

ShelteringTree.Earth, LLC Publishing
PO Box 973, Eagle Lake, FL 33839

Did you enjoy this book?
We love to hear from our readers.
Please visit the author at
ShelteringTree.Earth

About the Cover:

Artist Jerry Francis

Title of Piece Thirst for a Shiny Object

Location Private collection of Jerry Francis

On a walk in a forest, I came across a small brook filled with stones. It originated from a spring about 100 feet upstream and curved down a short steep hill into a wetland. When I admired the stream's beauty, the early morning sun broke through the tree opening, lighting up the stream and focusing on a small stone. As an example of the eureka moments in my life, I knew instantly that this was the painting of the brook scene that I should use as the cover *For the Good of the Order*. For additional emphasis, I digitally enhanced the single stone by using a slight star pattern and blurred both sides of the brook.

What is a "Dyslexic Friendly" Book?

Sheltering Tree Media has taken steps to make our books more friendly for those who live with dyslexia. While the following principles will not make every book readable for every reader, it is our best effort to create products that encourage reading and to support all readers.

Throughout the book, we use a font named OpenDyslexic. This is a free font that is designed to help dyslexic readers distinguish each letter from the others. For more information about OpenDyslexic, how it differs from other fonts, and research behind the font, visit their website: www.opendyslexic.com. In our book created for adults, we use 12-point font. This size font provides the reader plenty of spacing between the letters (which is called kerning). The bigger, wider font tends to be easier to the reader's eyes.

The space between each word is increased (this is called word spacing). This helps better distinguish when one word ends and the next begins. The line spacing is greater than most common fonts (this is called *leading*). This all should help with readability.

Whenever possible, the text is Left-Aligned but it is not justified on the right side. Allowing the right side of a paragraph to remain *rough* keeps the word spacing consistent throughout.

Our Dyslexic Friendly books are printed on cream or ivory paper which is also thicker than the average book page. This minimizes the sharp contrast of black-on-white pages as well as bleedthrough of text from the previous page.

Finally, Sheltering Tree Media has made colored overlays available when you purchase a book through our online store. You can find these overlays at ShelteringTreeMedia.com/shop/dyslexic-friendly.

These are some of the principles we use to create a book as readable as possible to those living with dyslexia. Some may find this helpful; some may not. Please provide us with any insights you might have to improve our Dyslexic Friendly principles. We pray this will enable many to heighten their love for reading.

DEDICATION

I dedicate this book to the good men in our local
Knights of Columbus Council who, with generous
hearts, continue giving themselves to those who
need extra help.

These selfless men have inspired me to dig deep
into my own story. They make me feel part of
the continuing burning flame of their journeys by
humbly lifting up even total strangers.

CONTENTS

INTRODUCTION

Remember the last time you left your faith-influenced meeting with a smile? More than likely, near the end of the meeting, someone said a joke or gave the group something positive to think about. If your group has old and new business, voting, and meeting minutes, then your gathering uses Robert's Rules.[1] A rarely used before adjournment possibility of Robert Rules called *For the Good of the Order* is the ability for someone to offer some kind of insight.

Years ago, I was tapped on the shoulder to see if I would be willing to take on the position of Lecturer for our local Knights of Columbus council. The Lecturer offers purposeful thoughts during *For the Good of the Order* at the close of monthly meetings. I said I would consider the position after doing some research. My initial search mainly found overview suggestions on how somebody could do this. These included one's insights, materials that might be available such as short videos or articles, and the idea of inviting guest speakers. Although apprehensive, there seemed to be material available. It should have been relatively easy to offer something encouraging each month.

I quickly discovered that preparing and delivering a monthly thought was not easy. For example, using a video would require excessive setup time. I also tried the article approach, but almost nothing I found seemed to offer positive reinforcement for the members present or fit the multiple tenants of our fraternal order. Since our meeting typically ended around 9:00 PM, my attempts to bring in guest speakers who first had to sit through our meeting to have 3-5 minutes to speak fell on deaf ears. I also tried some other ideas, but nothing seemed to flow smoothly. I felt lost in the position and was about to give up.

In desperation, I deferred to prayerful interior reflection. I was surprised by the surfacing of a simple response of just being myself. Not long after I began understanding what *being myself* meant, I realized that *For the Good of the Order* was also good for my well-being. It became apparent that without focused perseverance to become a better person, how could I possibly share uplifting stories with others? Initially, the task occupied a tiny portion of my life, but I began to live a self-fulfilling prophecy. Deep within my heart, I had discerned that I would have something valuable to others if I paid attention to my steps forward.

Within the first year, the zig-zag path forward for me to fully engage the role of Lecturer *For the Good of the Order* began to straighten out. I settled into a routine of primarily using my experiences presented as stories with an ending reflection for our members. I realized I had to make sure I needed to carve out time in the busyness of my days to think about what to say in the meetings. A few days before each meeting, I would compose my thoughts into the personal story I would offer. It was not long before that process changed to a wide range of how the stories would come together. At one end of the spectrum, I was usually beginning to think about what I might say in the next meeting immediately after the meeting I was just in. I also considered complex external events, so I knew I needed multiple options right up to the minute I was to speak.

The well-over 100 stories I have shared grew out of my desire to become a better man as well as to share more global issues. Most of the time, the stories simply acknowledge that feeling a certain way is ok and we are on the right path. From these numerous meeting experiences, I know there will always be something that resonates with one or more members. However, each time beforehand, I still pray and desire that hope's anticipation will drive my belief that the result will be good.

I have become relaxed with sharing what can be very personal stories with the men, and the preparation has become part of my everyday life. Interestingly, I had something good to say dozens of times long before a meeting. Occasionally last-minute circumstances that affect our organization become important. In these cases, I ignored what I had prepared and just went for it with nothing more than psychological readiness and a simple thought or two as a starter.

In this book, I share stories that most often reflect my profoundly personal journey toward being a person that met my definition of "For the Good of the Order." These stories come from what seemed like an endless pool of a lifetime of experiences. I have been metering them out about once a month for well over a decade. When I first wrote this book, it was initially intended for fraternal orders that include faith in God (in my case Christian) as a premise within the organization's charter. However, I have come to see that even if your organization does not reference the divine, providing worthwhile thoughts at the end of your meetings can be applied.

In each of your organizations, I believe a person capable of telling positive stories can benefit the group. I had to figure this out myself using the school of hard knocks. I hope that offering uplifting stories based on personal experiences will provide the catalyst for someone in your organization to offer their own personal and uplifting stories. Since the synopsis of these stories ends up in the meetings of the meeting, I have grown comfortable with asking the scribe not to include something. Typically, this is because my story may be deeply personal. If you also choose to share information that you would prefer not to end up in the minutes, I am sure your recorder will honor your request not to include those details in the minutes. One idea that was just suggested is that I will offer my own synopsis to the recorder.

I have found that the content of my stories is primarily irrelevant and soon forgotten. More importantly, the stories create a vehicle to trigger each individual's thoughts during *For The Good of the Order*. I am amazed how many times I have heard that someone had also been there and done that. Technically there is no way my story is the same as theirs. However, in effect, what it means is the person gets the analogy. The analogy's essence has been distilled from their heart to touch an emotion for that person. For anyone considering offering stories, I can assure you that because of their personal nature, people have been respectful and have not repeated any of mine.

What is wonderful is that I often hear them tell their own stories. It does not matter what your story might be, but I know these kinds of stories, animated with facial and body language, provide amusement and laughter as a great way to close a meeting. Laughter means that often missed valuable human emotions have risen to the surface. Laughter can heal minor wounds, break tensions in a group, and, best of all, warm from within.

I have learned to appreciate the courage it takes to be a storyteller who can share values about the good that can be achieved in our lifetime. This book contains stories in more extended form than I used in a meeting to give you more context because the members of my organization know me well. I have also included scripture that was in my thoughts during the process of putting together the original verbal version. These stories should not be interpreted as biographical or preachy but instead used to provide a possible concept for others. As a member-based organization, I hope you may find it beneficial to add an uplifting *For the Good of the Order* to your meetings.

DELIVERING A FOR THE GOOD OF THE ORDER

Our organization uses a modified form of Roberts Good of the Order. In Robert's version, items that can be included are disciplinary matters. I can appreciate the proper use of this time to help the organization deal with issues, good or bad, that make the order better. However, I have chosen to deviate slightly from Roberts Rules in that I do my best to use stories focused on the positives that can help uplift our organization.

Most of my stories use common, positive, uplifting emotions. These emotions are used as the titles of the chapters in this book. Each chapter includes three stories related to that emotion. The chapters are not meant to be in any specific order. Think of them as a guide for a type of story that might fit the mood for a meeting.

DICTIONARY DEFINITIONS FOR EMOTIONAL TERMS[2]

Altruism – Regard for others, both natural and moral, without regard for oneself; devotion to the interests of others; brotherly kindness. Action or behavior that benefits another or others at some cost to the performer.

Amusement – To entertain or occupy in a pleasant manner; to stir with pleasing emotions. To cause laughter or amusement; to be funny.

Awe – filled with wonder and amazement.

Cheerfulness – Noticeably happy and optimistic. Bright and pleasant.

Contentment – The state or degree of being contented or satisfied. Happiness in one's situation; satisfaction. The experience of fulfillment and ease in one's condition, body, and mind.

Enjoyment – The condition of enjoying anything. An enjoyable state of mind. An activity that gives pleasure.

Gratitude – The state of being grateful, appreciative, and thankful.

Happiness – The emotion of being happy; joy, prosperity, thriving, wellbeing.

Hope - To want something to happen, with a sense of expectation that it might. To be optimistic. To trust with confident expectation of good.

Inspiration – exercising an elevating or stimulating influence upon the intellect or emotions

Joy – A feeling of extreme happiness or cheerfulness, especially related to acquiring or expecting something good.

Love – A profound and caring affection towards someone. Affectionate, benevolent concern or care for other people and their well-being. A feeling of intense attraction towards someone. A deep or abiding liking for something

Optimism – a tendency to expect the best.

JOY

SHINY METAL OBJECTS

I am one of those people that is attracted to *shiny metal objects*. For me, it is a metaphor that I have come to perceive that almost everything can momentarily stop me in my tracks to admire its beauty. Using the idiom *forest for the tree*, I usually only see the entire forest. If you put a single tree in front of me, I will not see its details. When a tree suddenly becomes apparent, I pay attention because something about that tree (shiny object) will bring me joy.

When I need to reduce my stress levels or if I want to let go, I have learned to prepare myself to be ready to see detail. In other words, I become prepared to receive the gift of beauty with joy. This becomes quite obvious when I go on hikes into a forest. Certain conditions help focus my attention and let me recognize that I will lose my forest view and see a shiny metal object. On a hike like this, I become excited when I unexpectedly encounter a small brook near or crossing my trail. I become wide awake to details as I know that my favorite kind of shiny object will appear.

As silly as it sounds, I know I will notice a unique small stone among the many rocks in the stream. Sometimes it's a stone that is a different color than others. Perhaps the shape of the rock makes it stand out or because it glistens a certain way in the sunlight. I pick up that stone, and almost childlike, I admire its uniqueness. Most of the time, that stone goes into my small backpack. When I get home, it will go into a large plastic container filled with other stones that have caught my attention over the years. Before I get ahead of myself, that is another story.

For me, admiring a shiny metal object's uniqueness can have several meanings. By now, you may have realized that the stone has not called out to me. It is the moment itself that becomes important because of the joy it brings. If you could see the smile on my face when I simply hold a brook-washed stone, you would instantly recognize contentment and total surrender. At that moment, all is right with the world. Those few seconds are extraordinary because I have stepped back from my routine. Those things in my life, such as anguish, stress, and frustration, to name a few feelings, disappear from my emotions and senses.

Another observation is that the object does not even have to be shiny. For instance, I  enjoy restoring antique hand tools. There have been many times I picked up an old rusty tool that would be better off in the metal scrap pile. I get this innate interior feeling that I can bring it back to life. For example, I gently restored this Stanley brass marking tool to its original worn but usable beauty. Or I will notice the early budding of a flower, such as a rose, in one of my wife's gardens in our yard. You may know this expressed as taking time to smell the flowers (a type of shiny metal object). I get this look from her that I am silly, because I tell her that her flowers are budding. To her, of course, they are developing, as that is what flowers do; yet she knows I have had a moment of joy. I especially cherish these moments with her and others that may be with me in my heightened awareness of beauty because at the same time I feel the closeness to those I love. Saint Paul knew and spoke of the essence of taking the time to do so.

> Finally, brothers, whatever is true, whatever is honorable, whatever is just, whatever is pure, whatever is lovely, whatever is gracious, if there is any excellence and if there is anything worthy of praise, think about these things (Philippians 4:8 NABRE).[3]

I want to challenge you to find the time to seek your shiny metal objects. Step back from your regular routine to create a moment of awe and wonder. Perhaps like me, you can think back to those beautiful moments when you were satiated. Don't you deserve one of these moments yourself? Couldn't you find a way to put aside all your busyness to let the bits and pieces of glory that surround you fill you with happiness, even if it is just for a fleeting moment? You may even discover an internal desire to seek them out rather than waiting for them to find you. We all need a grounding, a touch point, or something that draws us away long enough from the constant demands of life so we can become refreshed sufficiently to take on our challenges.

FAMILY TRADITIONS

My father's and mothers' grandparents were of French-Canadian descent and immigrated to the US from Canada as adults. They grew up poor, with potatoes as a primary part of their diet. Their jobs paid very little during the Great Depression; potatoes became an invaluable portion of their diet. One such use of potatoes from the French-Canadian culture, called poutines, has survived as a one a year tradition in our family. As a child, I can still vividly remember the excitement of getting together with my grandparents and my father's brothers and sisters to make poutine rapeès (poutines).

In Canada, the more widespread use of poutine using potatoes is French fries with gravy. However, in southeastern Canada, a poutine (rapee) is a snowball-sized and colored mixture of mashed and grated potatoes with ground pork inside wrapped in cheesecloth to hold it all together, boiled thoroughly for a long time until cooked. Making our localized variation of lean pork-centered poutine is a tremendous amount of labor, so it takes a group of people to make them.

A couple of years ago, I did the math of the "manufacturing cost" of making a poutine. Even at minimum wage and ingredients, each poutine costs about six dollars. Not many people would be willing to pay six dollars for a potato meal that also requires an acquired taste to appreciate. A generation ago, a robust commercial market has dwindled, and the largest company that was making them went out of business.

When my grandparents passed, we still kept the over 100-year-old tradition alive by getting together once a year to make poutines. My father and his siblings, and a couple of cousins helped out in the process of making the poutines. Like any culture, French Canadians have their unique fun filled family gatherings. With this background, you can imagine the comedy of emotions involved in my family making poutines. Usually, the smallest batch size is 50 pounds of potatoes, producing around 40 poutines each about 3" in diameter. When raw potatoes are peeled or grated and exposed to the air, they almost immediately turn a dirty gray unappetizing color.

When my grandfather was alive, we grated the potatoes using an upright hand grater. The process was hilarious because what the freshly grated potatoes had to sneak under a wet cloth to join the pile already grated. If it was done quickly the wet cloth would keep the potatoes closer to white. As a child, I remember the constant refrain during the peeling process of "get those potatoes in the water!" At that age, it felt like the most essential thing in the world was to get that potato into the water fast enough. If you were quick enough, you were a hero.

In all the years I have helped make poutines, I have never seen one that was not some shade of grey. In my humble opinion, grey does not affect the taste or texture. Yet, everyone in my family dwelled on this impossible task. Looking back, I am very suspicious that they knew it was impossible, but tradition drove the family to these shared, joyful, and laughable emotions.

The grating was hilarious in comparison to the peeling. I have realized hand grating the potato resonated with my family's poverty and the value of every piece of that potato. If you have hand-grated before, you know the potato gets smaller and more difficult to hold. When this happened in our poutine-making process, we all knew the secret evidential ingredient was about to get into the grated potatoes. There was no time for complaining because of the need to get the potatoes under the wet dishcloth cloth to prevent discoloration. I can't explain it, but there would be lots of laughter at the expense of this process. Of course, no one but us knew of the secret ingredients created from our fingers rubbing against the grater. Making Poutines varies, especially in the meat used. This YouTube video is close to our version of a poutine other than that we use very lean pork and make a meatball out of the pork: https://www.youtube.com/watch?v=4q9Dyc6oUEc.

Looking back, I realized there was a little bit of me in every poutine, and I mean that physically and spiritually. After my grandfather died, we started using a grating machine. Now, the lack of the secret ingredient comes up in our conversations when we make a batch. When my father died, I took over for him, working with his younger brother, who still leads the once-a-year tradition of making the yearly poutines. In the silence of the past, I can still hear the refrain in my mind of getting the potatoes into the water and under the wet cloth so they do not turn grey.

The purpose in this entire tradition is to make perfect poutines to give to friends and family. Each poutine has already been designated for a specific person. These unique yearly gifts are a physical way of saying "I cherish you" to those who receive them. For the first time this year, we broached what will happen to the tradition of making poutines in the future. This is because the batch sizes are getting smaller. Older people who enjoyed the gift of poutines from us are passing. Very few of our children enjoy the acquired taste and rubbery texture of the potato with a pork meatball inside.

Some family traditions have been in place since recorded history. I have friends who celebrate Passover every year with a Seder meal. This tradition has been in place and practiced for thousands of years beginning when Moses created Passover as a Memorial.

> It will be like a sign on your hand and a reminder on your forehead, so that the teaching of the LORD will be on your lips: with a strong hand the LORD brought you out of Egypt (Exodus 13:9).

I have personally attended a Seder and it is a time to celebrate the past and a wonderful future together.

There is no question about the joy of getting together and having lots of fun. I look forward to the family tradition of making poutines because the hugging of my uncle, his wife and my aunt when my wife and I both arrive and leave reminds me of the larger gathering of grandparents, uncles, aunts and cousins of years before. Left unsaid is a sense of how we need to positively celebrate the thousands of poutines given away over the years despite the pending loss of this tradition.

The tradition of poutines is just one small example of how I am filled with joy from so many blessings in my life. Yet, as a man, there seems to be something in my DNA that affects my ability to fully, quickly, and freely express joy. Even if it is in each of our DNA, shouldn't we try to break free to let others see that interior joy?

BEING EMBARRASSED

Since I am in the woods so much, I have installed apps on my phone to identify mushrooms, trees, wild edibles, and amphibians, to name a few. In the last few years, my favorite phone application has helped to identify plants. I seem to notice something but do not know its name when I become acutely aware of my surroundings in the forest, or, in some cases, a plant I have never seen before.

Specific encounters seem to be instantly etched into my sub-conscience. I can still frequently recall one such moment shortly after I learned to forage edible wild mushrooms safely. I decided to go foraging for morel mushrooms, so I studied everything I needed to know before going into the woods. Prime locations include long abandoned apple orchards. I knew of one only a few miles from my house. After I fought my way through dense growth that had taken over the perimeter of the old orchard, I walked up to the first tree among many.

Right in front of me was a four-inch-tall  morel ready to be harvested. I really could not believe how easy it was to find one. I knelt to pick it up and was surrounded by a sense of being embraced back from the joy I felt. Many years have passed along with searches in dozens of orchards, and I found only one other orchard with morels. When I am feeling down and need a little nudge, that morel experience is one of the dozens I can think of to get a sense of a joyful embrace.

On vacation a few years ago, I walked along a deer trail about half a mile from the nearest house. Right where the path turned sharply, I noticed a plant I had never seen before. I used the plant app on my phone to determine I had encountered an endangered, very rare wild orchid in full bloom. Being from New England, I knew the more common type orchid of Lady Slippers. Like the morel mushroom experience, I was supposed to look at details at the right moment. Once I knew it was so rare, I whispered thanks for the opportunity to view such beauty. I had another moment I could treasure for the embrace that came with it.

These more spiritual types of embraces differ from those of my wife or a friend. However, like physical embraces, they seem to bring a sense of peace and comfort. I can remember long hugs with my wife with as much reverence. These bonding embraces are especially important in shared times of sadness or deep-felt joy. I know that I am receiving just as much in these embraces as I am giving.

I have male friends who enjoy a short embrace and genuinely look forward to it. With one of my friends, we sometimes, on purpose, touch our heads to each other. I easily recognize that my friend is saying I am vulnerable, and I deeply enjoy sharing my time with you. I can honestly say I feel likewise. I can recall those types of embraces differently, but they also bring me peace and joy. I also smile when I see other forms of how strong an embrace is.

For many years we heated our house with a wood stove. I truly enjoyed doing it because it got me outside working with trees I had cut down to clear land for our home. Those trees yielded a decade of heat. I was given a bumper sticker that read, "Have you hugged your wood stove today?" I put it on the back of the stairs that go into my cellar where the woodstove was. I still smile when I look at it and think of the apparent silliness. St. Paul plainly tell us that we can know these embraces as fruit of the Spirit.

> [22] the fruit of the Spirit is love, joy, peace, patience, kindness, generosity, faithfulness, [23] gentleness, self-control. Against such there is no law. (Galatians 5:22-23).

All of these embraces remind me that it ok to enjoy and treasure you give and receive.

CONTENTMENT

COLLECTIONS

I fondly remember my first stone as a shiny metal object from a brook. We lived in a small town for the first dozen years of my life. I would get on my bike with my fishing pole to catch and release native brook trout at a local brook. These tiny fish are smaller than the length of your hand yet are one of the most challenging fish to catch. As in other shiny metal objects, you must genuinely understand a native trout's environment and be completely invisible to them so all they see is your fly.

Several days after a heavy rainstorm, I went to the brook to fish. It had become swollen over the sides and then receded, washing away the topsoil to expose an expanse of stones I had not seen before. The sun shone brightly, and the beautiful palette in front of me included a thumbnail-sized piece of fool's gold. Over the years in that town, I collected a small box filled with fool's gold and other shiny stones such as mica and pea-sized garnets. When we moved to another town, I was disappointed when I realized my mother decided this box of rocks was worthless and threw it away.

Our move was to be to a more populated town. In my early teens, my collections turned to baseball cards and stamps. I clearly remember how fun it was to do. We moved again in my late teens, and a shoebox full of baseball cards and a stamp collection did not seem to have value, so they were given to my younger cousins. You can probably tell there is another story brewing within this story.

Years later, when I married and built a house in my early 20's, my collections became more permanent. I even dedicated space in the cellar for them. However, my collections grew with those shiny metal objects without realizing it, branching out to things such as beach-found driftwood. Likewise, my book collection is massive, spanning multiple bookcases, and has recently overflowed on the floor because I never knew when I would need them. Quite a few books are associated with my graduate degrees, so in my mind, I may need them for business or pastoral ministry. I often do abstract paintings of something I have seen. They end up in one of the boxes of the many other paintings I have done, which has overflowed into a third box.

My most extensive collections are those things I need to maintain my house. These also use up the most space. For instance, I have a 30-gallon barrel filled with all sorts of tall objects. This includes old broken broom handles. I have many partially filled paint cans that we used to paint the rooms of the house. I opened one up the other day, and it was half-filled with solidified paint. Most of these paint cans are obsolete because the room was repainted with another color.

As I approach retirement age, I am beginning to see many of my collections are useless. I have reluctantly started to sort out things that I now realize I will never find a use for them for the rest of my life. There is a harsher reality of my endpoint. I had an epiphany about collecting antique tools gathered from yard sales that require ten six-foot-high shelves. While my collections are neatly organized, I doubt they will have future value after my passing other than as a token reminder that I was an orderly collector bordering on being a hoarder.

These are not morbid thoughts; they are natural maturing of a measure of success that, in truth, is valued by only one person: me. I have started to bring my excessive items to the town transfer station for recycling. I have a new sense of contentment. I can see that each collection has filled voids in my life. The wonder of hindsight has revealed and prevented me from seeking a feeling of worldly success. My contentment is because I no longer need these inexpensive, harmless collections. In my own way I am following

Jesus's advice:

> ³³ Sell your belongings and give alms. Provide money bags for yourselves that do not wear out, an inexhaustible treasure in heaven that no thief can reach nor moth destroy. ³⁴ For where your treasure is, there also will your heart be (Luke 12:33-34).

If you look back at your life, you may find that you have a measurement of your worth outside of money, and you are happy with that sense. If not, then maybe you can find a way to let go of what is no longer needed to fill those past voids in awe of the person of wonder you are.

ANIMALS

Some of you may have had a pet as a child and may have one now. As a child, I did not, but my next-door neighbors had all types of farm animals. I distinctly remember that the only difference between how they treated their farm animals, and their family dog was that the dog was let into their house. Otherwise, their farm animals seemed to want to be near them just as much as the dog. Each animal was named and came to them when called. Most of the time, the animals knew my neighbor was present, even if silent. I fondly recall times when they came to me during my daily visits.

It seemed to me that their farm animals could also be considered pets as these farm animals were well cared for and received individualized attention. I know first-hand that my neighbor friends knew their sheep, and the sheep knew them in the same way Jesus knows us and we know Him. *My sheep hear my voice. I know them, and they follow me* (John 10:27). When this relationship occurs, a bond is developed, including contentment. I know I felt at ease around these animals because they trusted me.

When my wife and I built our first house, we got a cat because her family had grown up with cats. Our first cat was a thin stray cat living outside on a farm. No matter what we tried, as soon as a door was cracked open, even just a little, she would invisibly run out. She also had the bonding need to find a male cat so she could have kittens. None of our neighbors had a cat, but somehow our cat got pregnant. She was a friendly cat, and as soon as you sat down, she would be on your lap, contently purring, knowing somebody would pet her. In the latter days of her pregnancy, she would crawl into our bed, positioning herself so her face was against one of us.

When our cat became pregnant, I knew I had to create a safe place for her when she had her kittens. Since I had experience with my neighbor's cats in my youth, I knew I had to put an open cardboard box with a soft cloth on the bottom in a quiet darker place in our house. Whenever our cat would nuzzle up against me, I would put her in the box, then walk away. Within a minute, she would be back on my lap, and the cycle would continue until she stayed for a few minutes. Nevertheless, I thought I had trained her to use the box when ready.

Unfortunately, her trust and contentment with me to use the box when she had the kittens did not work. I woke up suddenly one night with a slimly wet kitten on my face. Despite all my effort, my cat wanted me this close to her at this tender moment. Since the bed was already a mess, I did not have it in me to move her into the box, so I let her have her other kittens on a towel on the bed while I sat next to her, petting her. The next kitten that came out, she licked it clean, then pushed it closer to me, expecting me to help her take care of her kitten that quickly. It was a fantastic moment as I had never experienced this amount of closeness with an animal.

Now, I have chickens, and they also have personalities. Some are ultra-friendly and can't wait to be petted or held. All of them are right there, ready to be near me, when they hear me come towards the coop. When I enter their run, I am sure to bring a treat, and they are all over me to get their share. While I know the pleasure brings them to me, the trust keeps them there. I do not treat them like house pets. Yet, there is a high degree of enjoyment and contentment, knowing I am taking proper care of these animals while at the same time harvesting fresh eggs for breakfast every day.

With all types of predators around, I built a portable run to move around the yard during daylight. They are in the run in under a minute, ready for the day's journey. I can hear their cooing, so I know they are happy. Watching them, I notice their personalities and feel peace and comfort in caring for them. While not pets, I have to be honest and admit that they still bring joy and contentment to my life. When I reach under them in their nest to get eggs, they rub against me, telling me it is ok. Doing this, I am sometimes surprised by thoughts about that first cat having laid a kitten on my face. I am filled with contentment, knowing I have learned to care for these animals properly.

Caring for animals is only the first rung of the contentment ladder. When caring is understood as more than a responsibility, it is easy to see that it extends well beyond ourselves into society. If you think about who you care for, I suspect you have a sense of internal satisfaction and contentment. Contentment has a lasting effect and draws us out outward. It is one of those signs that we are fully human.

LUSTER

We all have things that we do that bring us to a place in our minds where we are relaxed. One of my favorite hobbies is restoring antique hand tools. Antiques, in general, are a moving target because what may have been vintage 25 years ago is now an antique from the passage of time. The tools I like to restore are those before the advent of chrome. The outer layer of a modern tool includes copper on top of the underlying steel, followed by nickel which adheres to the copper, then chrome, which adheres to the nickel.

I like tools from the period of only copper and nickel plating. Nickel is not as shiny as chrome. Shiny, for me, is a relative term, so perhaps the word luster is more appropriate. Luster is also a relative term like beauty is in the eye of the beholder. Every object can have a luster as it describes how bright or polished the outer surface is. For example, the sun can turn a small stone in a gently flowing brook into a shining object because the water acts as a polishing agent. When you take that stone from the stream and let it dry, it becomes an otherwise indistinct stone. The surface sheen disappears to reveal the actual surface.

Old tools have the same characteristics. It becomes a useless tool without a solid inner layer hidden under the surface. If you go to the store today to buy a tool, you will see that gleaming ultra-thin chrome layer. You have no way of knowing the strengths and character of that specific tool. On the other hand, when you pick up an antique tool, the outer layer of nickel and copper disappears from use over time. More often than not, because there is no longer a coating on the surface causing the exposure of the iron or steel layer, the tool has become rusty.

At one end of the spectrum of restoration is to do nothing but wipe off the dust to display an old tool in its rusty condition. At the other end of the spectrum, people use an aggressive technique such as a wire wheel to remove the rust, even going as far as re-plating it with nickel. I am more in the middle, using a gentle organic, non-toxic technique to remove most of the rust without affecting the tool. Doing so reminds me of the person using the tool over their lifetime, during which most of the shiny outside would be naturally gone.

Despite the outer surface that the tool is missing, I have realized that it is still fully functional in the craftsman's hands. Due to my experience restoring hundreds of tools, I can attest that there is a noticeable difference between the underlying metals in the antique tool and a modern tool stripped of its outside surface. The metal in most modern tools is not designed to last generations because the metals are softer and less durable. A new cost-saving strategy only uses suitable metals as inserts at the edges of the tool's primary function. The metal on the balance of the device bends and breaks quite easily. As little as one generation from now, these modern tools will effectively be useless.

That outer luster removed from modern tools quickly exposes weak inner layers. When that rust layer is minimized on an antique tool, you are still rewarded with a solid inner layer that will last many generations. Rather than putting a new surface on an antique tool, I restore it to its unique luster. While this means the tool will not reflect light in all directions like a chrome-plated polished tool, it still has its luster. This luster is the kind that endures.

We can take this metaphor to describe the luster of people. We all know people who want to appear to be bright and shiny. When we get to know some of these people, we can be disappointed by their observed inner weaknesses. We know people who have a solid moral compass but less obvious luster. Some may naturally be that way. I am sure you know others who have been refurbished to expose their true inner strengths. Taking the metaphor a little deeper, we could say the people who have put on that thin outer perfection layer make their appearance shiny and likely self-centered. The people who do not need a polished surface are those whose true selves offer themselves to serve others. Jesus warns about showing our outer surface instead of who we really are:

> [3] Therefore, do and observe all things whatsoever they tell you, but do not follow their example. For they preach but they do not practice. [4] They tie up heavy burdens [hard to carry] and lay them on people's shoulders, but they will not lift a finger to move them. [5] All their works are performed to be seen. They widen their phylacteries and lengthen their tassels (Matthew 23:3-5).

From personal experience, I have had that thin veneer of shine showing off as a technology guru without much interior sharing skills at one point in my life. I continue to be restored with values and attributes that are more humble, compassionate, and caring for others. This is perhaps why restoring antique tools is ideal because I am being put through the same process. I have my luster, and so do each of you. Your luster is as shiny to me as any polished chrome object because I witness your inner worth.

AMUSEMENT

CHILDREN

Years ago, I helped lead a scout group of teenage boys for a week-long hike of nine 4000-foot-high mountains in the White Mountains of New Hampshire. With very few exceptions, the hike was hilarious at every turn. The boys always had something going that made the few adults involved chuckle. Each evening we slept in tents on designated platforms across the mountain range. For more than half the trip, we were on the Appalachian Trail (AT)

This location allowed us to meet people called "through-hikers" as they attempted to hike the entire AT length. The White Mountain section of the AT is considered one of the most challenging sections. By the time the hikers reach the White Mountains, they have traversed over 80% of the nearly 2200 miles of the AT. They have accumulated a confident attitude about the finish line by this point. It was apparent to me they were most interested in resting, getting some nourishment, and getting well-deserved sleep. With these teens ready to pounce on them, that was an impossibility.

It would take less than fifteen minutes before the boys would get the AT hikers to open up about their hike and often their reasons for the adventure's months-long commitment. The boys wanted to know everything. In the first couple of days, their questions were mainly about the physical effort of hiking the AT. When the boys started hearing similar answers from various hikers the boys became bored. About half through our reaching the peaks of ten mountains the boys had multiple days experience of hiking. The boys knew the actual uncomfortable side effects of hiking long distances. They began sharing what they knew with the AT hikers. It was incredibly entertaining, especially with the woman hikers. The combination of teen boys trying to outdo each other with the young adult woman through hikers was like nothing I had observed before.

The most asked questions were related to the human body, and of course, food intake and outtake topped the list. The boys did not mind asking the same questions to the multi-day hikers who hiked the trail in sections. The boys quickly figured out the formula of questions that got the most laughs. The beauty of these moments was precious because the boys never crossed the imaginary morality line, which could have quickly happened in these conversations. We came to know more about a particular phenomenon ourselves. Within the first three days, we discovered that the human body processes freeze-dried foods differently than regular food. What happens is that the digestive system has to work overtime, which creates a lot of unexpected gas.

The boy's goal became who could have the loudest noises from the gas accumulation. They could not wait for the evenings to get the through-hikers to join in what seemed like competitions. The boys got so bold with their noises that we heard them talking about saving up for when we got to the tops of the mountains. We planned most of our day around reaching the summits during mid-morning through late afternoons to be at the campsites well before dark. Our late afternoon arrivals at the mountain summits meant we met up with day hikers that climbed a single mountain. There were times when there would be as many as 50 people gathered at the summit of one of these mountains.

Being a person of faith, I would step aside to pray, staying within earshot if needed. After a late afternoon arrival, we reached the summit near the end of our week. Since our hike was mainly circular, this lofty summit had a view of almost every mountain we climbed. It was a stunning panorama, and I felt tremendous gratitude. I found a spot to pray a short distance from people who had just summitted the mountain. In the background noise, as I entered silent prayer, I could hear the laughter building from what the boys were doing. Out of nowhere, one of the boys let go and yelled at the top of his lungs that his sound was the best one he had ever made. The mountain exploded with joyful noises of congratulations and laughter.

Here I was, immersed in prayer while simultaneously participating in fantastic amusement of what was happening. I will never forget feeling just in the right place at the right time. I was allowed to simultaneously mingle the human and divine with the amusement at the moment that seemed intensified by an order of magnitude. I was reminded of who I was in one of Jesus's lessons about children.

> At that very moment he rejoiced [in] the holy Spirit and said, I give you praise, Father, Lord of heaven and earth, for although you have hidden these things from the wise and the learned you have revealed them to the childlike.

Yes, Father, such has been your gracious will. (Luke 10:21).

While some might think this experience was crass, I realized it could have easily been a missed opportunity. I often think back to this moment when I am in other oddly amusing situations and no longer have to wonder if God is present. Perhaps you can let your guard down a little and allow amusement to multiply within. You may find that you can move from a simple smile to joining in the laughter. From my practice in doing so, I know these experiences can re-energize you.

GAMBLING, DINING OUT, AND PARTY MINIMALISM

Being amused and enjoying laughter is an often-missed valuable human emotion. It is an emotion capable of minor wound healing, breaking group tensions, and warming from within to refill our well. However, we must maintain internal limits to how much we balance our self-serving desire to be fulfilled with the desire to be part of our earthly community. The expression "everything is ok as long as it's done in moderation" comes to mind. However, moderation for one person may have different boundaries for another person.

There is a relatively new concept called minimalism. Its history dates back to the early 1900s when a Russian artist painted a small black square on a white canvas. This could be considered the absolute far end of the scale in terms of a painting. In the 1970s, it evolved from art into all facets of life. One concept was the idea of not going beyond the satisfaction of minimal personal needs. Like many new phenomena, the definition of minimalism has morphed and changed over the years to be considered extreme.

Another way to interpret minimalism is to be aware and conscious of the decision-making of your time, talent, and treasures. This perspective of minimalism has a particular meaning on the faith-based purpose of things in life such as doing for others as you would want them to do for you. There are other premises of the roots of the Christian faith. Jesus's Parable of the Talents comes to mind regarding what we do and the results of our Gifts from God:

For to everyone who has, more will be given and he will grow rich; but from the one who has not, even what he has will be taken away (Matthew 25:29).

In this context, any faith-based organization committed to helping others in physical or spiritual needs can be considered minimalist because of its focus on what others need.

Being happy with your choices and expressing the universal voice of laughter is part of not being excessive. This does not mean we have to give up everything. In my humble opinion, it is ok to briefly touch the edges of something that might ordinarily fit outside the lines of excess. For instance, if my wife and I go out to dinner, we rarely spend more than $70 in the entire evening. That includes an appetizer, meal, drinks, and an occasional dessert. To keep in balance, I feel comfortable if I spend the same amount of time praying or doing volunteer community work.

Likewise, you might think that going to the casino might be off-limits and outside the definition of minimalism. However, we go to a casino once or twice a year, each with a $20 spending limit. Our $20 usually lasts an hour or so at the slot machines. Within that hour, we both had enough to satisfy our curiosity. To be honest, neither of us can fathom how someone could sit in front of one of those machines to spend so much out of their paycheck. When we occasionally end up with more than we started, we give the rest away one way or another.

When I was in my 30's, I was on a business trip to Asia. While waiting for my associate at the hotel, I put a $1 token into one of the slot machines arranged in the hotel's open spaces. From that one token, I ended up with almost $1000 in less than five minutes. We left for our meeting, but later that day, I purchased a pearl necklace for my wife at a significant discount from a friend's father's jewelry store. It was my first large-value purchase from a situation like that.

That purchase triggered an awkward attempt to give away the balance while in Asia, but that is another story. The combination of the win, purchase, and the failure at how I tried to compensate continues to awaken the learned experience. It was the first and last time I truly felt the need to want to be at one of those machines for very long. I must admit that I enjoyed that winning moment in Asia then. I still remember laughing all the way to our meeting with my associate. My lesson became that it was ok to be at the casino with a reasonable amount of money I would typically spend to entertain and have fun. This single event grew into my attitude of trying to avoid excesses.

I have attended parties where alcohol is flowing. Early in my adult life, I discovered that if I have more than a couple of drinks in an evening, I will have a massive multi-day migraine within a few hours of drinking. Using another idiom, I have a natural aversion and a built-in *governor* that prevents me from drinking to the point of even getting a slight buzz. To explain a governor, in the 1960s and

70s, parents could put a physical device in their car that governed and prevented the vehicle from going over a particular speed for their teenage drivers. The concept of a governor is still in use today. Governors now take on other shapes, such as electronic ankle bracelets for low-level criminals to have a limited daily time in society.

It seems we can create our natural governors when we attend parties. Since alcohol tends to loosen our inhibitions, we should be able to detect when our drinking has reached a point where we think we have more freedom to draw outside the lines. My line is knowing if I have another drink, I will suffer far more than a simple hangover than is worth to keep drinking. In one way, you could say that I am lucky. Interestingly, I have found I can still have as much laughter, fun, and amusement as anyone else that may be drinking too much. In other words, I would challenge you if you find yourself ready to draw outside the line to consider not having that extra drink and see if you can continue to have fun.

I have learned to fit in with everyone else by holding onto an empty beer bottle or have the bartender give me a glass of something non-alcoholic. I remember the first time I made this suggestion at a company planning meeting to entertain an important customer. It went over like a lead balloon. However, I know firsthand from friends who have tried this experiment that having a little wiggle room is possible.

They have learned that they can still have a couple of drinks and enjoy the evening to be amused along with everyone else. From experience, I would like to suggest you give it a try. You may find it just as liberating to be minimalistic when avoiding excess at parties.

CHILDREN AT PLAY

Years ago, when my children lived at home, I always enjoyed watching them do something. In the yard doing chores, I would take the time to visit them because it would make me glow inside without them knowing it. I could tell their minds and bodies were engaged, and I would feel thrilled when I encouraged them to explore deeper into what they were doing. When I found that one of them liked something, I would help them broaden their scope.

Sometimes this meant having them join a group such as a baseball team or scouts. My wife and I would also join these groups not to keep an eye on them but to watch them grow with the other children. Then there were times I knew nothing about the subject or was not capable of helping them. I fondly remember my oldest daughter loving music. My friend Australia was moving back home and offered the piano he'd bought for his daughter me at a meager cost. I knew my daughter, who was four then, would love it. From the minute the piano was in our house my daughter was at the piano every day until she left for college,

My youngest daughter also did the same. My daughters took filling the house with music and constantly amusing my wife and me by putting on concerts and shows. I could not help either of them with music because I am pretty much tone-deaf. However, I can still hear that piano playing in my mind and the joy it brought to our home. It has been silent for years, but my youngest daughter just purchased a house, and it's going there to make many more years of beautiful sounds for her own family. I am thrilled both of them still enjoy music despite my ability to help them only as a cheerleader. I did what I could to allow them to explore and grow.

Giving my children the opportunity to do so with groups was just as fun. We would go to the play park, and they would play with the other children until we said it was time to go. When the climbing bars became age-appropriate, I would show them how to do it, then assist them until they could do it themselves. Even after they learned something, it was rare for me not to be nearby to observe and show appreciation. Children watching one of my children would want to do the same. I would glance over to their parents to wait for the nod to let their child do so.

As soon as their children would do something new, there was cheering, clapping, and giant smiles on those parents' faces. This continued to be true while my children grew older. I was a cub scout leader, then moved into scouts to help create adventures in our monthly camping trips. I have many memories of all the beautiful moments in scouts. It was truly amazing to be part of these opportunities to help my children and their friends try new things and move forward.

I also remember looking at parents who watched while leaders helped their children have fun while learning something. I could tell these parents were entertained and amused. I felt disappointed when some of the parents were engaged in talking with other parents that they missed their child doing something the child had never done before.

For one of our activities, we had over 30 boys go ice fishing at a nearby pond, and I had invited parents to be there because we would have a bonfire and be out on the ice to fish and skate. I had over two dozen ice fishing tilts and two ice augers for the scouts to use. There were a total of only six adult scout leaders and parents there. We set up the first tilt and had just started to set up the second tilt when the flag went up on the first tilt. The boys all ran over, and we proceeded to bring in a nice bass.

There was laughter all over, and the boys wanted to keep it. I said we would put this one back and make an aquarium by digging out a big trench in the ice so the fish we caught could swim, then we could release them later. Some boys just enjoyed watching and feeding the fish worms in the aquarium. They joyfully and gently put them back in the ice holes. At the same time, we kept trying to set up the rest of the tilts for hours, but the fish just kept coming before we could.

I had brought five dozen shiners as bait, and we ran out of bait even before we had all the tilts in. It was truly an exciting day with the kids constantly moving around catching fish. The laughing and joy never stopped the entire time. It was non-stop stunning amusement by and for all. Unfortunately for parents that did not go, they missed out on bonding with their children through fun times like this.

Now I am a grandparent, and I can repeat it all over again. My 3-year-old grandson is incredibly amusing to me. Since he loves to be outside, we have many incredible adventures together. I smile each time as he affectionately speaks of my daughter's new baby boy as "my baby brother." The thought that, as a 3-year-old, he already sees his role as big brother warms me from the inside.

These moments when we engage with children and behave like them allow us to recall the many scenes in scripture when Jesus calls out our capacity to serve others (including children). My favorite passage is in Mark when Jesus takes a child into his arms:

> [35] Then he sat down, called the Twelve, and said to them, "If anyone wishes to be first, he shall be the last of all and the servant of all." [36] Taking a child he placed it in their midst, and putting his arms around it he said to them, [37] "Whoever receives one child such as this in my name, receives me; and whoever receives me, receives not me but the One who sent me." (Mark 9:35-37)

Being present in an amusing way with children or adults builds a lifetime of memories. No matter what happens in our lives, we can bring these memories to the surface to bring smiles to our faces.

ALTRUISM

GENEROSITY WITHIN YOUR ORGANIZATION

One of the four tenants of the KoC organization is charity. For our specific council, charity is distinctly the primary focus. We have a truck trailer retrofitted to become a food truck. At various times of the year, the food truck is used for Friday fish fries. It is also there for the town's annual Chain of Lights for freshly made fried dough.

This food truck is unique because the volunteers contribute their time, talents, and treasures. 100% of all the profits are used to help others in need. You would think this alone would be a sufficient amount of charity for the individual members. Many people who spend time on the food truck also do the same for other charity fund-raising events. The events include an annual golf tournament, helping out at a social action ministry, and providing dry goods and seasonal produce for the local food panties, to name a few.

Our members could easily be doing something else, yet they are dedicated beyond any standard measurement of charity. I constantly witness their adjustment of personal schedules so they can jump in and help someone in need. In all the years I have been a member, I have never seen a member expect anything in return. It is inspiringly unique that they are not alone in their commitment, as their spouses are highly supportive. When someone thanks them for their effort, all I ever hear in return is a humble, "you are welcome." A visible fire is inside each, displayed in their constant smiles, joy, and laughter.

At our meetings, there is always a flow of ideas to improve the ability to provide for those in our community who could use a little help. There is always respect for each other's views, ages, beliefs, abilities, and disabilities. In the meetings, the primary motivation is charity, without the need for anything in return for the member's effort. What these members are about and live for precisely fits the definition of altruism.

You might ask yourself why one should try so hard or even try at all? You may know others at the opposite end of the extreme who do nothing beyond token donations to get a tax break. Honestly, it is hard to break free from a routine and step into the shoes of those in need. You should not be embarrassed or ashamed for doing something beyond your comfort zone. This feeling has to come from within our hearts and thoughts. St. Paul speaks eloquently of this: *Each must do as already determined, without sadness or compulsion, for God loves a cheerful giver* (2 Corinthians 9:7). Generosity is a sense of being fully human in heart and mind and the possibility of sharing yourself with others. This means you have discovered that some of what you have for time, talent, and treasure belongs to someone else. It could be helping and sharing yourself with family, close friends or people you may not even know.

I have met people who instantly recognize within a single sentence in a conversation that they could be doing something more for others. When I have these conversations about generosity

I make it clear I am talking about an opportunity that focuses on the future. I never mention the past. If you know how about being generous conversations, there must be no contempt for history but instead support the present. Otherwise, the human emotions of regret and fear along with not being good enough will get in the way. We need to support and praise those moved to help others. This is the truth of altruism, as it is not an easy transition and can take years. If you are already altruistic, let that show in your actions, not in a badge or words.

TO BE RICH IN SPIRIT AND TRANSFORMATION

My small software company is focused on the management and consumption of knowledge. Our customers are large companies and organizations with extensive distribution of staff that need knowledge on demand. That focus took an interesting twist in 2005 through a collision of circumstances, I donated a copy of my company's software to Habitat for Humanity, an international Non-Governmental Organization (NGO). When I got involved with Habitat, I realized other NGOs were helping the worldwide needs of those who needed help. Each NGO had the same problem of sharing knowledge and educating their employees and volunteers. Most NGOs aim to ensure they stay at or above 94% use of their funds to help others. This means that their entire operating expenses need to be below 5%.

After thinking and praying about the dual problem of helping others and minimizing NGO expenses, I decided to donate our software to these other NGOs. I approached Habitat to reach out to discuss this idea with other similar NGOs. This first conversation led to Catholic Relief Services (CRS) agreeing and accepting the use of our software. That resulted in a rippling set of calls to other NGOs and an individual who had just retired by selling his software company. He was already working with a few NGOs on the reuse of knowledge strategy. He had already been working with an individual at Save the Children. She was there while on a sabbatical from her role as an executive responsible for education at a large software company.

What started an idea to donate my company's software to Habitat created many related situations that flowed remarkably fast.

In under three months from the introduction by the original NGO, our little all-volunteer team engaged in conversations with over a dozen large NGOs such as World Vision, Heifer International, Save the Children, and the Nature Conservancy. Within a brief period, these conversations resulted in the founding of a small all-volunteer non-profit called Learning for International Non-Government Organizations (LINGOs) based on the principle of the reuse and sharing of knowledge among the staff and volunteers of international NGOs. I am humbled that I was a corporate founder and board member of LINGOs for six years. It became an incredible example of NGOs and businesses working together with donated products and services.

As a board member, I witnessed over 90 NGOs becoming members of LINGOs to use the platform conceived with just a few conversations. Our efforts dramatically reduced NGO training costs returning the savings to places such as villages in need worldwide. Through these NGOs, I firsthand witnessed extreme poverty. Listening to how these NGOs served the needs of millions of people sometimes brought me to tears. You would think that helping to form a non-profit that helped these organizations to reduce operating costs to put the savings they use would have the most significance for me from this effort. However, there was something even more significant. My Christian insight created a different viewpoint on the transformation of wealthy people involved in these organizations. I saw their genuine concern and desire to help without any personal gain. I heard countless stories of the hidden pull of their heartstrings from these people.

To this day, I remember seeing these transformations and still hold my time with LINGOs in my heart. I genuinely enjoy telling the story, mainly focusing on the time and talents of everyone involved. It was a personal acknowledgment of knowing something greater existed outside of myself and those who participated. It does not matter what you want to call it, but to me, everyone, including those wealthy, allowed a spiritual event to happen. I am still stunned that I could be with those who, long before meeting me, loved their neighbor well beyond themselves. This incredible treasure drives me as I continue to progress in my journey.

But the story does not end there because this entire effort happened at the exact historical moment when the values of the top one percent were being called into question. Due to what I knew could be a false narrative, I became curious about other wealthy individuals pouring themselves into helping lift others out of poverty. For instance, I knew that Bono of U2 has helped raise over a billion dollars for aid to Africa. He started the ONE movement with the support of Pope John Paul, which resulted in many countries forgiving four-hundred-billion dollars in the debt of third-world countries. AIDs is down dramatically in Africa due to people like Bono.

Bill Gates, one of the wealthiest people in the world, formed the Giving Pledge, which has attracted over 175 billionaires agreeing to spend the majority of their wealth on philanthropic efforts. While I do not agree with some of the philosophies of Bono or those who joined in the Giving Pledge, it is evident that they are having a movement of the heart. This same movement that is happening in a large number of wealthy people is also the closing of the story of Zacchaeus in the Bible:

> [8] But Zacchaeus stood there and said to the Lord, "Behold, half of my possessions, Lord, I shall give to the poor, and if I have extorted anything from anyone I shall repay it four times over." [9] And Jesus said to him, "Today salvation has come to this house because this man too is a descendant of Abraham (Luke 19:8-9).

If the hearts of those who have significant wealth can be changed, it should be easy for the remainder of society to do the same with their time, talent, and treasures.

THE APPLE DOES NOT FALL FAR
FROM THE TREE

Along the line, in my early adult life, I started to accumulate metaphors, parables, and idioms. I suspect this is because I found myself moving in the direction of computer technology. I did not realize it, but I would frequently use one of these idioms to explain something in terms that non-technical people would understand. This went well until I entered a technical marketing position with many people who were not natively from the U.S. Almost immediately. I noticed blank stares when I had a conversation with them. It did not take long before I realized that using metaphors was the issue.

There was one instance that was striking. I spoke to a small audience about how we would handle a big mistake that *slipped through the cracks*. We needed to quickly resolve it because the *barn door was left open*. Those of us whose native language is English would have understood that *slipped through the cracks* meant something had unintentionally not been noticed. The *barn door was left open* meant the horse bolted from the barn and needed to be returned home. Imagine what you would have thought if you had never heard these phrases. Wouldn't you have a blank stare?

One woman in the group from a large city in France took me aside to ask about what I meant. Once I explained each one, she said there were similar idioms in France. Then she did something remarkable. Since the group would work together for a while, she talked to her boss, who approved her purchasing a book with idioms. It had many U.S. English phrases equivalent to several other languages for everyone in the group. She thought so highly of how I explained the technology that she adopted the technique and convinced others to do the same. Not long afterward, they all felt comfortable using their own countries' idioms, and I needed to rely on the book myself.

She had unselfishly shown concern for others and reacted positively toward helping them. To this day, I remember this moment, not wholly because of the idiom book but because I could recognize even in the business world that, we can have concern for others when they need help. From that point forward, I have learned that when I notice I am using an idiom with someone I can tell is not getting it, I fully explain it. When doing so, I repeat the book story and the explanation. The laughter can sometimes be *heard for miles*.

In this experience, not only did the seed of the apple that fell from the tree produce another similar but unique tree, causing a ripple effect. As you can see, the idiom the apple does not fall far from the tree fits outside of usually how it is used. Most of us use it to observe how a child often has some of the same characteristics as a parent. This is the case with my children, as I see each of them helping others uniquely. I have witnessed many people caring for others, and I am sure if you have children, you can appreciate passing on the responsibility of sharing what you have with others.

My technological background has continued to evolve because technology is in constant flux. As a young adult the entire scenario that developed at my job of using a book of idioms opened my eyes to the possibility that I had freely shared my knowledge. Using metaphors was the beginning of figuring out that I was also an educator.

I have come to believe that the idiom moment triggered me to create my own company. I often recall how I did so in the early days of the internet web to focus on using technology to educate others. My desire to teach led me to be a team leader of teen faith formation. Not long after starting my company, I became an adjunct professor and developed the internet and intranet courses for my state's university. Without realizing it, I had gone down *the road not taken, with arms wide open* to mix all these seemingly disparate elements in my life so that the apple tree could blossom and let more seeds take root.

I suspect metaphors have been used since the beginning of human communication. Consider Jesus's use of idioms and metaphors to emphasize what he meant in His role as a teacher. Many of Jesus's metaphors survived the 2000 years of history to our modern times, such as: *Should anyone press you into service for one mile, go with him for two miles* (Matthew 5:41). The version in use today is to go *the extra mile* which means in effect, to do more than what is expected.

Jesus was met with many blank stares and needed to take the time to explain what he meant. I have adopted this same strategy of using an idiom in my attempt to explain something that I knew others did not understand as well as me. For over two decades, I have *tuned into* groups of people *going the extra mile* to help others. Tears have sometimes flowed from watching and participating with those who have very little to multi-millionaires who have and continue to be ready and willing to help the world by creating a rising tide that floats all boats.

INSPIRATION

VISUALIZATION INTO REALIZATION

Many years ago, I had a wonderful experience in prayer in which I mentally visualized a happily married couple with their hearts bound together with a beautiful rope. I was reminded of these thoughts while dining with my in-laws at Christmas that year. I had made turkey saltimbocca roll-ups tied with colored twine. As I was serving it, the scene of the couple came to mind.

In a few seconds of looking at the twine, I realized that it was composed of fibers twisted into many separate strands. A single thread can easily be broken but becomes stronger when combined and united with others. Later, I realized this could be taken further as a metaphor for marriage, self, family, and friends.

It's probably not hard to imagine yourself as a single fiber able to break at any instant. Now think instead of how you have braided yourself with others creating an enduring rope. Each time someone bonds with you the rope becomes stronger. The rope as a metaphor is expanding in breadth and depth.

Think about when things were not perfect with one of your relationships, and that fiber broke. Doesn't your rope remain strong despite what might have happened in that relationship? It seems that for our ropes to have strength, we should always be reaching out with our fiber toward others, even to total strangers. This simple view of the possibilities of strengthening myself by becoming a working member of something else has inspired me countless times to push myself beyond my comfort level. I have successfully taken on a task that, when I look back, would not have been possible if my rope was not strong enough.

Taking the analogy one step further, if the things we do are done magnanimously, it is possible to envision the rope morphing into a more substantial material like steel cable wraps. What if that cable could become a mega-cable used with other mega-cables to build a bridge reaching toward the beyond to a world of unlimited possibilities? Imagine your single fiber anchored at one end to your grounding and the other end free to connect to goodness, exploring human values and righteousness.

I often recall the famous inspirational quote from pilot John Magee that President Reagan immortalized.

Oh, I have slipped
The surly bonds of earth...
Put out my hand
And touched the face of God.

Perhaps pilot John Magee flying upwards in the perceived perfection in his flight has left us a message. In-flight, John Magee was still grounded and solidly tethered at one end to his life here. He could not fly that plane without being built by others, maintained for safety, or guided by flight controllers. That is what it can be with enduring relationships that allow us to safely abandon our fears and be inspired to reach out beyond our fibers to do our part to strengthen our world.

There are others like John Magee who have inspired us to proceed forward boldly. The work of Mother Theresa continues to bring millions of people into her vision. As a young man, I was among an entire generation inspired by Martin Luther King Jr. to treat everyone with kindness, compassion, and love. Dr. King's striking "I have a Dream" speech in reference to these values includes one of my favorite quotes in all of Hebrew Scripture.

Every valley shall be lifted up,
every mountain and hill made low;
The rugged land shall be a plain,
the rough country, a broad valley.
Then the glory of the Lord shall be
revealed,

and all flesh shall see it together;
for the mouth of the Lord has spoken.
(Isaiah 40:4-5)

Many others have led me to the truth of our need to be united and bound together, not broken down into our fibers. While we may not have the same skill, time, talent, or treasures as well-known inspirational people, we can do our part. To perceive and believe in our inspirations has no less value in helping to bring the good of the other to the surface. Honestly, I have people very close to me that inspire me far more than these famous heroes of inspiration. Perhaps you also have that same situation. Maybe you can meekly let them know how much they inspire you.

COMMITMENT TO DO

The original intent of this book was to share a written version of some of the stories I used to help conclude monthly meetings of our local Knights of Columbus council. I thought it made sense to research the history of the KoC and present it as a review for the council members, I discovered a commonality that a few people often form organizations like the Knights of Columbus. We can compare our beginnings within an organization to the founder's vision as part of our identity. One way to do so is to formulate those beginnings into a story that can be told of those who committed themselves to the action of that organization's "To Do" moments.

For example, the first meeting of the KoC occurred over 120 years ago. Gathered were 24 men, including the founder, Father Michael J. McGivney.[4] The history of the KoC begins with a small group of Catholic men witnessing significant opposition to immigrants, especially Irish Catholics but also Jewish people and those facing racial discrimination. The KoC began by addressing this opposition with charity by helping local immigrants in numerous ways beyond Father McGivney's spiritual responsibility. His local KoC supported a small portion of the Irish immigrants who had come from Ireland to escape a famine in an attempt to feed their families and the hope of better circumstances. The timing of an influx of Irish immigrants happened during an already tense period in the United States. Immigrants were looked down upon as invaders, removing jobs and services from those already in the US.

Most Americans were still recovering from the Civil War. Many had relatives and family members who had served in the war and lost husbands and family members. They were in desperate need and felt there was no room for these immigrants to take the already low number of jobs.

The KoC rapidly expanded in small councils throughout the US, continuing to support immigrants and others affected by discrimination and needing help. Immigrants worked as farmhands, building along the railways and as factory workers. Taking these jobs from those already in the U.S. led to rampant discrimination against the rising population of immigrants. There were also significant efforts to disrupt these immigrants by rejecting their beliefs and principles. One of the most intense disruptions for immigrants in the decades following the Civil War was threats from the Ku Klux Klan. The KKK targeted populations and took violent actions against all who opposed them. The KKK led a campaign against the KoC because it supported not just immigrants but the KoC's stance on equal rights for decades. These actions directly affected Fr. McGivney as his home church building was burned to the ground. None of these numerous setbacks deterred Fr. McGivney and the mission of the KoC.

The early history of the KoC has many firsts. These include the first blood drive in the U.S. and a growing organizational focus on the dignity of life. The four tenants of the early Knights of Columbus remain today in the form of fraternity, charity, unity, and patriotism. Father. McGivney could only participant in a short period of the KoC's growth because he died at the age of 38 due to his exposure in his youth working in the toxic environment at the local brass factory.

We are proud and respectful of what Fr. McGivney started and continue in the tradition created by this group of 24 men. What he started is a reflection of Jesus' commission of the disciples.

> [7] As you go, make this proclamation: 'The kingdom of heaven is at hand.' [8] Cure the sick, raise the dead, cleanse lepers, drive out demons. Without cost you have received; without cost you are to give. [9] Do not take gold or silver or copper for your belts; [10] no sack for the journey, or a second tunic, or sandals, or walking

stick. *The laborer deserves his keep*
(Matthew 10:7-9).

The disciples initial effort expanded,
continuing with St. Paul, and now over 2000
years as people and many charitable
organizations do the same.

Over 16,000 small worldwide KoC councils
mirror that first meeting of Fr. McGivney and
the 24 men. While the efforts of individual
councils are small, added together with all the
other councils, the impact of charity reflects
the nature of the beginnings. For instance, our
country is always in the process of influxes of
immigrants. How we deal with situations like
this is a tricky question. If we consider the
compassion of Fr. McGivney, then perhaps, we
can help find solutions that satisfy both sides
of the equation.

RECOGNIZING HEROES

Veterans Day was coming up, and our Grand Knight approached me with the idea of a Patriotic Rosary. We each looked for a Rosary that would match the values of our organization but could not find one that did so. I took on the challenge since I lead the Rosary before our monthly business meeting and have written alternate scriptural Rosaries. A Rosary is a prayer tool to help use the sense of touch to focus on the Trinity of Father, Son, and Holy Spirit. It consists of repeated use of the prayers of The Lord's Prayer, Scripture, time for reflection, and the Hail Mary, which asks Mary to pray with us for Jesus's assistance.

At first, I played with the idea of using historical armed forces people who had faith in their ideals. However, I realized I was missing the mark of a broader understanding of patriotism and the heroes that make it possible. As I did more research, I had an *ah-ha* moment to look up the dictionary definition of what it means to be patriotic. I learned that being a patriot does not belong to a specific type of person or any particular period.

Instead, it is a belief that we can all come together around the underlying principles of freedoms and rights that have previously been won but still need to be maintained. These freedoms and rights are often centered around a constitutional republic in a democratic tradition, so it is not limited to the United States of America. Being patriotic is a shared obligation by those responsible for governance, those now or previously in uniforms, educators, clergy, and each of us as individuals.

Veterans serve as a prominent, clear symbol of patriotism. I genuinely believe that we will not truly appreciate others in all we do without God participating in our lives. Once I sorted out these thoughts, I put together a Patriot Rosary that mingles an acknowledgment of being patriotic with a love of God, who unconditionally loves everyone.

I started to think about the broad categories of people who put themselves on the line to represent these values. These people include Christians, our leaders, and those who dedicate themselves to keeping alive the idea that faith can bring clarity to our daily work and family lives. Since this rosary was going to be used in a Catholic ceremony, I specifically thought of the Catholic spiritual leaders of the Holy Father, Bishops, Priests, Monks, Nuns, various silent Celibates, Chaplains, Catholic educators, and all those who pray for our "One Nation Under God."

Numerous veterans have quietly put themselves on the front line as heroes defending our nation's values. For instance, my father served in the military toward and after the end of World War II. After WWII ended, he and many other men and women in their teenage years silently stood for our nation in extreme rebuilding tasks worldwide. I am proud that my father and other young veterans brought hope and freedom to those starving and suffering in concentration camps. His story is one of the many others who served at this time and other historical conflicts. Veterans day allows us to reflect on veterans' tragedies, especially veterans suffering from mental health, spiritual and physical wounds.

Then there are the patriots in the federal and local branches of government responsible for protecting freedoms within our Constitution and Bill of Rights. What of the heroes we encounter daily in the various types of public service workers such as police, firefighters, and health workers. There are many other heroes, such as those who keep constant watch and assist in maintaining the dignity of children or the elderly. I am confident you can come up with heroes in your life. Keeping them in your thoughts and prayers connects you to them and prepares you to become a hero, even if only for a moment in your specific situation.

AWE

SOMETHING TO SUSTAIN US

Even after her passing, Mother Theresa's commitment to the poor resonates with many others because of her efforts. Something that intrigues me is that early in her career, she had a mystical experience that sustained her for the rest of her life. This awestruck moment gave her everything she needed to become herself. Maybe not so substantial, but I believe we all have moments to reflect on. Each time we do, they encourage and sustain us in various ways. I have such a moment to share with you.

I typically wake up before dawn, so I have seen my share of beautiful sunrises that remind and inspire me each time. In Maine, on vacation, we stayed at a lake house that faced east. The house was slightly elevated above the water, with a fabulous view of rolling hills across the lake. It had a small dock extending into the lake. One morning as I looked out from the dock, I could see the sky begin to lighten, and almost immediately, clouds turned deep purple with a narrow golden stripe just above the rising sun. In less than one minute, the clouds flamed red, turned pink, and quickly transitioned to a typical blue sky. I watched in amazement during this unfolding process while a thin golden stripe formed for a few seconds then disappeared across the rolling hills.

Of course, at 5:30 AM, no one was out to see this crazed man kneeling down on the dock with arms raised, thanking God for the most glorious sunrise of his life. I knew in that instant that its beauty would sustain me when things were tough. As the vacation days started to go by, I could not help but go to that dock each morning to watch a more normal simple ball of sunrise above the tree line. Towards the end of the week, I woke up earlier than usual and had this overwhelming feeling to go out to the dock with a flashlight in the still pitch-black morning.

I grabbed my camera and a chair to sit in the silence and stillness on the dock waiting for the sunrise. I could not believe it, but the morning was opening like a few days before. I sat ready with the camera solidly locked in both hands, somehow knowing I had a chance to take a photo. I cannot find the words to describe the experience adequately, but I somehow captured the perfect moment with my camera in those few precious seconds. I

 witnessed an even more awesome sunrise than I had seen a few days earlier. The golden strip was thicker, the brightness viewable but not enough to turn away, the purple and orange were deeper in color, and the reflection spanning the entire lake was stunning.

I now possess a story of beauty and awe I continue to share and will treasure for the rest of my life. I have sometimes recalled it to get me through some rough-edged times. I have lost track of the number of times that I have pulled the photo up on my computer screen to keep the darker moments of my life in check.

To be honest, I know this was just a superb sunrise. It was not a mystical miracle like Saint Theresa of Calcutta had. It was not just meant for me to contain it but rather to let it loose in conversations. My expectation has waned, but somehow I thought I might see a sunrise that surpassed this glorious one. Now over 15 years later, that sunrise is still the best I have seen. It represents still yet unseen possibilities of powerful emotions that touch the center of my heart. This sunrise gives me hope for the wonder and awe that surrounds me.

If we allow ourselves to perceive the wonders in front of us, we will have a minuscule fraction of the awe Mother Theresa must have had. I have had many other awestruck moments, such as mountain scenes or witnessing an extremely rare endangered wildflower in full bloom just because I was on the right trail at the right moment in a forest. These incredible moments can stay in our memory to be recalled whenever we need them. God is a constant light shining on us, whether day or night, removing darkness from our thoughts.

> Thus says the LORD,
> Who gives the sun to light the day,
>   moon and stars to light the night;
> Who stirs up the sea so that its waves roar,
>   whose name is LORD of hosts
>   (Jeremiah 31:35).

I use glorious scenes in my life as a complete treasure chest or individually as stories to help others see they have wonderful treasures in their memory to get them past their situations.

BEAUTY

Furniture is generally built with veneered wood. The outer layer is a thin, perfect surface glued to less quality-looking but higher-strength wood. Much of what we touch and see has a veneered surface. Think of paint that protects a car or the paint on the walls of where you might be right now. If you drink coffee like me, your teeth get that light yellow stain that does not come off. Toothpaste that whitens your teeth with brushing only partially works. To get back to the standard white for their teeth, some people choose to apply a veneer that covers up the yellow staining or decaying teeth.

If you think about it a little, most things we know are veneered are physical. I want to catch you off guard for a moment to challenge you to think about how you express yourself in different groups. Don't you craft your views to be accommodating? When you do this, isn't it a type of veneer to present a moderated picture than what you may feel? I know I do it almost unconsciously, so I do not appear to be confrontational.

When we look at an artist's work, we can have a sense of the art speaking to us somehow. The colors, brush strokes, or object shapes can make the thin coating of paint on the canvas have incredible depth. It makes us consider what that artist thought, how they did that, or how long did it take. We can become interested in the artist. For example, my favorite artist is *James Tissot*.[5] Somehow, he created detailed mini masterpieces with watercolor paint on canvas smaller than a sheet of paper. I became so enamored by his paintings that I decided to learn about Tissot's childhood.

I use James Tissot's works almost every time I speak of the concept of beauty. If I had not looked under the veneer canvas surface of his paintings into the man himself, I would have never known how many similarities I had with him. When I did so, there was an intense, beautiful moment when I realized what mattered in my life: I needed to start spending more time exploring the beauty inside people. For me, the veneered surface of a person's skin, size, or hairstyle is always transparent, so I can more easily reveal the beauty of their inner self. My thoughts resonant with Saint Peter's preaching on the subject:

> [3] Your adornment should not be an external one ... [4] but rather the hidden character of the heart, expressed in the imperishable beauty of a gentle and calm disposition, which is precious in the sight of God (1 Peter 3:3-4).

What has become essential to me is discovering the solid base behind the veneer that makes the person who they are. What typically happens for me is exploring the intensity of how the love of neighbor comes to the surface for them. To me, internal love and beauty have become synonymous. A few years back, at a teen retreat, I discussed the subject of beauty and love with them. I pointed out how easy it was to look at a person that, through no fault of their own, had facial surface blemishes, and we unconsciously avoid that person. It was easy to use acne as an example, and some teens do not want to be seen with that person. I went on to describe other things we do that are significantly surface-related.

Then on purpose, I shocked the entire room by looking one of the teen girls right in the eyes silently for a couple of seconds, then said, "I love you." Almost every teen gasped. I went silent for a few moments to let it sink in. Without any reservations, I began to tell them how beautiful I thought each of them was. Again, there was a stare of disbelief as this older man seemed to be admitting what a strange person he was. I felt the room tense, which was the exact reaction I was trying to achieve. I then began to describe this sense of the desire to know what is under the surface of each other.

At the end of my discussion, I could tell I had hit a nerve and made them think about the true nature of beauty because of how loud the clapping was. I noticed almost immediately that after that presentation, they were comfortable conversing with me. I have done this again since, and I believe they would keep this concept in their minds every time.

There is certainly beauty in the veneered surfaces surrounding us, but more importantly, it is under the cover of all those we encounter. Isn't it interesting that when we speak of love, it is within our heart, an internal organ that cannot process information like the brain?

COMET KOHOUTEK AND
THE NORTHERN LIGHTS

Some of you might remember hearing about the ability to see Comet Kohoutek in early 1974. I had not yet known of it then, so I was surprised one late afternoon when looking out a window to see what I thought was a slow-moving asteroid. With Kohoutek's long orange glowing tail, the setting sun, thin clouds, the height of the building, and where I was positioned all made Kohoutek look spectacular.

But Kohoutek is not really what I remember. Instead, I remember the courage of a girl my age who must have repeatedly seen me visiting that window with a mountain view. I was still an immature teen, and, at that moment, I did not think much of it. She stood beside me to introduce herself, telling me she liked looking out the window. As she did so, we witnessed perhaps the best view of Kohoutek that almost anyone had seen. Its color, angle to us, and the extraordinary length of the tail seem better than the pictures Nasa took from space. What we saw together confused the scene because this girl I had not even noticed took a chance to be alone with me.

This moment complicated my life because my favorite pastime was being alone in the quiet of a deep forest. I thought God might be calling me to be a priest, monk, or brother at a Catholic religious order such as the Carmelites. Because of this, I had only been on a couple of dates. Despite my internal dilemma, I asked her for a dinner date. Cars back then had front bench seats, and after our meal, she snuggled up to me when we got in the car. Combined with how we met under the rarity of the astronomical event sealed the deal that God was telling me something: I could not deny that the embrace of a woman in my life was meaningful.

I occasionally think about that Kohoutek moment because it was a primer for a far more significant out worldly experience. The second astronomical event overshadows the first, but they go together because of their similarities. My family decided to move to a new town. Not long after moving, I met my future wife at a party at the college she was attending. The more time we spent with each other, the more comfortable I felt about our relationship. Not long into our relationship, I remember having a wonderful time together, and it was late. I remember saying our goodbyes with a long hug and a meaningful kiss.

I was still thinking about it as I pulled into my driveway. I opened my car door to stare into a sky-filled Aurora Borealis, extremely rare in our latitude. It lasted for about a minute. It was the most visually exciting thing I had ever experienced. The shimmering greens and blues combined with the wave-like movement were unbelievable.

This event happened before the advent of cell phones with built-in cameras and text messaging. In the first few seconds, I wanted to call my future wife but did not do so because it would have woken up her roommate. I did not want to call my best friend and everyone at my house because it would have also woken them up in the middle of the night.

I should have done so because I had not known its rarity. The next day I started telling everyone about it, and no one believed me because no one else had seen it, and it was not reported in the paper. Seeing Kohoutek and Aurora Borealis were both possible because the spot I was standing gave me that view you can have with a rainbow. Sometimes, someone right near you cannot even see the rainbow you see. However, I know what I saw with the Aurora Borealis. It was not an illusion. I researched the phenomena at the town library (no internet back then!) and found that seeing the Aurora Borealis where I live is extremely rare but possible.

None of that matters because a more critical thought arose from my awestruck night sky experience. I connected the dots to pay more attention and care more about the college girl I was dating. Because of the similarity to the first event, I took it as a sign that I could not mess up this blooming relationship. I have to admit I was a young man with no experience on how to proceed forward, and I made a lot of mistakes and, as a side note, still do.

In the next couple of years, while we both went to college and got to know one another, our seriousness about our relationship morphed like a butterfly emerging from a cocoon. We decided to get married, and I have not looked back. I have seen many other incredible events that remind me to recognize signs. Not all signs are celestial like mine or the Three Magi:

[1] When Jesus was born in Bethlehem of Judea, in the days of King Herod behold, magi from the east arrived in Jerusalem, saying, [2] "Where is the newborn king of the Jews? We saw his star at its rising and have come to do him homage." (Matthew 2:1-2)

Divine signs subtly surround us, and we can cultivate an instinct of watching for and discerning them to help point us in the right direction.

OPTIMISM

STEWARDS OF THE LAND

Many summers ago, I visited a friend in Maine who, like me, studies mushrooms, forages and eats the choice edible ones. He has learned to live off nearly 100% off the land. He has carefully managed his property, which includes using wild mushrooms he has cultivated in unexpected ways. We sat down to drink a homebrew beer, in which he substituted bitter mushrooms for the hops. Initially, I was hesitant because I thought putting mushrooms into beer would be weird, but it tasted excellent.

I was curious, and he enjoyed answering my curious questions about how he was primarily able to live off his property. At one point in our conversations, the subject of our stewardship of the land came up. My thoughts drifted to Genesis:

> Then God said: Let us make human beings in our image, after our likeness. Let them have dominion over the fish of the sea, the birds of the air, the tame animals, all the wild animals, and all the creatures that crawl on the earth (Genesis 1:26).

We discussed what God may have meant by giving us dominion over everything. At the time his views were much more grounded in the physical aspects of protecting and nurturing what we have than mine were. At the time, my own thoughts were more oriented toward the spiritual aspects of Genesis. Being an open-minded person, the takeaway from our conversation led to me adding to my own experiences of feeling that consuming God's gifts without rebuilding interrupted the definition of dominion for me. I became much more aware that a measurable percentage of our dominion was out of balance.

A few weeks later, my wife, daughter, and I went to Quabbin Reservoir in Massachusetts to take in the beauty at Enfield Lookout. The view was glorious, and we enjoyed being together to take it all in. After we walked back to the parking lot, I stopped to read the background information at the kiosk on how the reservoir was built. The scene from Genesis again flashed in my mind. Relating it to what I viewed at Enfield overlooking the Prescott Peninsular let me understand that sometimes even when we temporarily disrupt the environment, we can get it right in the rebuilding of what has been done.

Unfortunately for this area, Boston had a challenging political, economic, and future water need. The decision was made to destroy an entire town, parts of other towns, and properties from central Massachusetts to Boston for the aqueduct. This need for water disrupted thousands of people's lives while building the reservoir. I have to believe this was an extremely difficult process for these people, especially those displaced from their homes. Luckily, despite the building of the Quabbin happening decades before the broader acceptance of environmental impact, the forest surrounding the Quabbin reservoir is exceptionally managed. All kinds of wildlife, including bald eagles, bears, and the occasional moose, make it their home because of the care that went into restoring our *dominion*.

This thinking process of caring for our dominion is deeply embedded within my psyche. To this day, I constantly remind myself about the rest of the fifth day of Genesis when God is pleased: *God looked at everything he had made, and found it very good* (Genesis 1:31a). To me, that means what was good, while in flux, needs always needs to be good or, at minimum, quickly restored to good. I still vividly remember filling my lawnmower gas tank shortly after the visit to Enfield. I found myself making sure the cap was tight on the gas can, and the spout was in the tank so the gas did not spill out. I knew that if I spilled a thimbleful, it would only be a few cents worth. However, there is also the raw truth that thimble full is not cleanly absorbed into the earth. You could argue that some of it still ends up where it started as oil. Not being a scientist, I cannot disagree with that. To this day, I am still cautious with gas, occasionally reflecting on that single visit with my friend that locked in the desire to do so.

For the most part, most of us are now considering these thimble examples of stewardship for our environment. We recycle our paper, plastics, metal, and glass. We are making a dent in otherwise burying it in the ground for the next generation to figure out what to do with it. We are also restoring our rivers to their original beauty. In my teens, my family was living near the Nashua River. As I looked out my bedroom window at the river, the effects of the papermill upstream which manufactured color paper were evident.

As a teen, I remember making a big decision one rainy day when I saw the water flowing a grey-green color. I knew I had to get involved in the challenge to do something about it, but that is another story. For now, I can tell you the river flows wonderfully clean. There was a significant effort using federal funding and a massive effort by thousands of people to return the river to its original beauty. Trout that now live all along the river's length prove how clean and oxygenated the water is. This restoration process, among others, gives me a high degree of optimism that we can continue this march toward proper environmental considerations.

I recognized the relationship between God's meaning and where I needed to be. I know each of you also does your part to hope we are cautiously and adequately caring for the land. We have been designed to properly consume the earth's resources; however, every action has an opposite reaction. Our response must be to think about what those small thimbles of gas spilling into the planet might do.

I believe that we have to be careful not to shame each other into this concern. We cannot use a sledgehammer when a gentler tap from a jeweler's hammer will do. Others should not be forced but allowed to learn willingly, so they can see that we need a vision and path to managing our dominion. I am optimistic that humanity is humbly capable of honoring the gift of earth's land so that future generations can enjoy it the same or even better way we now do.

BEING SUNNY

As you know, our life events are sometimes like the weather which can be challenging to predict accurately. For instance, today, when I left home to go to work, the weather forecast was sunny, but it rained instead. My lunch break plans were to get outside for some fresh air and sun, so I could walk around the block to help reduce work stress. I was initially disappointed with the rain, but the umbrella in my car came to mind. When I decided to walk in the rain, I started relaxing, and the *rain inside* turned into sunniness.

Another example of being sunny despite my initial desire is that recently I had a neutral attitude when my wife and I went to see a theater performance of **The Sound of Music.** I could have never guessed that I would enjoy myself well beyond expectations. My perspective completely changed when I noticed the love story was also a history story. The historian in me surfaced, and I can still remember that moment when a change of perspective turned my attitude sunny.

I am just like everyone else in that suffering affects how we behave. I must actively mentally push constant pain aside to present myself correctly. It comes down to the fact that if I do not practice what I preach, how can I honestly reflect on how I would like to appear instead of how I might feel in the moment? It does not matter to me that I constantly fail but rather that I continuously try my best. I work hard at an outward cheerful disposition to signify who I am rather than let the physical surface.

I am often amazed and encouraged by others that put optimism and outward-facing joy first. Their smiles are genuine, but in many cases, I know their behind-the-scenes stories.

They know how to make room to bring their fun and positive feelings to the front of who they are. I am sure you all know people like this. If you ask them, they will tell you how they do it. I have, and it has brought great joy to my life when they share their stories with me.

I occasionally find myself heading toward a funk over some negative thing that is going on in my life. A trigger for me is when I see a significant, blatantly selfish act. It is like a chain reaction starting with having feelings of sadness that the person had probably been conditioned by outside influences to be that way. To break these funks, I bring to mind those people I know are not selfish and happy despite everything. It takes a little time, but I feel the selfless memories take hold so that everything can return to normal sunniness. I become like the man Jesus has made peaceful.

As they approached Jesus, they caught sight of the man who had been possessed by Legion, sitting there clothed and in his right mind (Mark 5:15a).

I have laid bare my hidden feelings to give you some potential clues about how you might find ways of being sunny yourself. I acknowledge that moving towards real happiness both inward and outward is not an instantaneous response, but I believe it is worth it spiritually and physically. I know that excess negatives take a toll on my body as during this time, my brain is producing chemicals such as adrenaline, pushing my blood pressure higher. Spiritually I know it is better when my friends and family see me with a sunny disposition.

RESETS

Business associates know I work hard to be a righteous business owner treating employees, partners, and customers equally. Whenever I recognize that I have created a situation that I have made unpleasant for someone, I apologize. When I talk about something that is wrong, I am always honest and factual. This makes for a good situation as I can be a sounding board when someone wants my reaction to a business dilemma that they may have.

I had such a scenario happen a few years ago when a business associate had to make a tough decision because of a flaw in a project. His decision process of what to do because of what happened would require him to spend about the same amount of time and money on what to do. He has to choose between dramatically correcting the project or restarting what he thought was nearly complete. The options he had thought of were all righteous and morally correct. I could not offer him any better options than he had already determined, but he still had to pick one.

I was a little reluctant to mention prayer to help him decide because I did not know him well enough to know about his faith. I took a chance and suggested it. I could tell by the expression on his face that prayer was not part of his routine. He said he would think about it, and I left it at that. A couple of weeks after we saw each other, he smiled and thanked me for suggesting prayer because he said it gave him clarity on which way to go. I never asked, and he did not volunteer his decision. What I detected in the conversation was that he had become optimistic that his decision of what to do was correct and that he would be able to do a reset.

The results of this encounter have led me to encourage prayer in my communications with business associates. This sense of encouragement in open communication has always been my desired style, whether business or not. I am blessed that my business associates, especially fellow entrepreneurs, try to apply optimism even in great difficulty.

In today's environment, there are many hot-button topics. You do not always know how someone might feel about these topics. When I find someone with a contrary opinion, I sometimes ask if they would be open to discussing other people's viewpoints. I avoid going direct because my perspective might be opposite theirs but instead try to lean towards using facts, imagination, and idioms to be more comfortable in conversation.

If there is a significant difference between my opinion and theirs, especially if it is a yes or no topic, I have to decide if I have the facts and not just feelings to support my viewpoint. Emotions are what most often get in the way of honest communication. I have also found that it is best to save how I feel to the end of the conversation instead of presenting it initially. We can turn to Saint Paul speaking to Romans for guidance regarding openness to conversation and judgment:

> [3] The one who eats must not despise the one who abstains, and the one who abstains must not pass judgment on the one who eats; for God has welcomed him. [4] Who are you to pass judgment on someone else's servant? Before his own master he stands or falls. And he will be upheld, for the Lord is able to make him stand (Romans 14:3-4).

I am happy with how often I can open the other person to consider the ramifications of their beliefs and perhaps even soften their hard stance. When I get the person to examine a different view, I put these kinds of conversations into my bucket of *big picture resets*, not as victories but as examples I can call upon in the future. What is essential is not the topic but how the other person's considerations became moderated rather than what could have become heated.

I have learned the hard way because, with my learning disability, my thoughts and sentences can come out in the wrong order. The saying *words are important* always haunts me because I mess up more often than I would like. It is challenging and disrupting for my desire for openness and patience to reach my point slowly. Unfortunately, that can cause significant rippling. It has even happened with someone very close to me. In one case, I did not mean to say something in the way it came out, and my apologies seemed to carry very little weight.

It took a couple of months of trying and prayer before the situation was quietly resolved without fanfare. I know I am not alone because it is common for people to truly not mean what has come out of their mouths. We must reach deep inside and be optimistic that whatever happens will be resolved, and time will help with the rest of the relationship. Knowing you have a situation that will have to have a reset can give you negative feelings but think back at those that worked. Each of them can be used to raise your optimism that all will be well.

LOVE

RECEIVING LOVE

I admit I was a little reluctant to have children of my own. I could get into the litany of reasons. I think it comes down to the fact that some of us had parents that had difficulty expressing their love in words. As a young man, I had not yet fully understood the language of unconditional love. I just was not sure if I knew how to love children properly. I look back now at my children, and I cannot believe how much I love them. Since we share the words of love, it leaves no doubt they love me. I cannot believe how blessed I am in all facets of my family and marriage. Honestly, I thought with all I had learned that I knew what love meant. Little did I know I was to learn love had more dimensions than I understood.

Knowing the value of love changed for me when I attended a men's retreat weekend. Over the weekend, there was much to learn about being a man of faith, but the major takeaway was that I learned how to receive unconditional love for the first time in my life. I had never been taught what complete unconditional love was, nor did I figure it out independently. The retreat leaders were able to show in stories and examples with our small group of men what it meant. To understand this type of love, we had to truly appreciate what people did for us when it was clear there was no reciprocal expectation.

The idea of no expectation is much harder for some of us than you might think. All my life, I thought it was fair to believe that the love that I gave would result in the person I gave it to would give me an equal return. The retreat taught me that in my past, if I did not get back what I put in, then I was drawn away from relationships that could have been wonderful. On the one hand, missing out on what could have been was devasting for me. On the other hand, I discovered I could instead appreciate the gift of unconditional giving and leverage my new knowledge of receiving more gratefully.

Shortly after attending the weekend, I called my mother with courage I had known available from deep within. I told her I loved her for the first time I had ever remembered. I could sense the surprise in her long-delayed reaction, but she, too, told me she loved me. It did not end there, my birthday was only a few weeks later, and she called to say I love you. My father had died a decade before, and unfortunately, neither one of us had said *I love you* to each other over his entire life. We had expressed appreciation for each other, and I remember him saying he was proud of me. Now I can put it in my writing: *Dad, I love you.*

This simple insight that love does not have a return obligation has made me a far better man. I no longer expect to need anything back when doing something for someone else. I am ecstatic when I get a *thank you*, and I now respond with a humble thank you. I have been moved in dramatic ways by being part of unconditional love. It is a sensation that I have never grown tired of having.

But wait, there is more! As a man in my late forties, I could count on a few fingers how many times I cried. Only once do I remember letting anyone see my tears, and that one time was with my wife. You may think real men do not cry, but I no longer buy that. Obviously, there is a time and place for letting tears show.

Interestingly enough, crying when you know love is present is contagious. After I learned to cry, I kept track by counting the times for a while. I stopped doing so when I realized crying had become more accessible. By then, I figured it was a permanent part of me, as I had reached a point that I thought seemed excessive for tiny things.

I can vividly remember being in a line of cars at a stoplight when a beggar with a rag was wiping the windshield of each vehicle, expecting some money in return. I reached into my pocket to retrieve a dollar for him. I opened the window, and when I handed him the dollar, he looked at me straight in the eyes. I received one of the most genuine "God blesses you" I could have imagined. I will never forget that first time. Not long afterward, my wife and I stopped at a fast-food place on the highway. She was not hungry and had an extra burger after leaving the highway. She handed me the burger at a stop to give her burger to a beggar because she said he was hungrier than she was. I finally realized this kind of love was second nature to her. I unconsciously turned away to hide the tears from her. When I regained my composure, I vocally acknowledged how wonderful what she had just done was.

I had not realized that in nearly forty years of marriage, the language of unconditional love growing inside me was already part of her. There have been other times I have wept however brief. It is an outward sign of love expressed by Jesus in one of the shortest verses of scripture: *And Jesus wept* (John 11:35). You may discover it if you don't know the sensation of unconditional love and are willing to be open to its subtle clues. Who knows, without excuses, you could join the growing group of real men who do cry.

PAIN IS NOT THE OPPOSITE OF LOVE

If you have ever broken a bone, you know that weird feeling that something is moving that should not be. Over the years, I have broken enough bones to learn that there are several types of bones where little can be done to help hold them in position while they heal. When you go in for an x-ray on one of these broken bones, the results will be that the doctor will tell you to wrap it and try not to stress the area. If you have had a cast, you know that it does not take long for the pain of those kinds of breaks to go away. That is because the bones are firmly held in place to heal, preventing nerves from signaling pain to the brain.

A cracked rib is not set in a cast so that even if wrapped, every movement causes you to wince. I had broken a rib in my teens, so recently, when a log had fallen into my ribcage, I knew immediately that had at least two cracked ribs. There is an interesting phenomenon associated with people with a cast. People see the physical sign and are immediately careful and caring. With broken ribs, no one can see a cast or wrapping.

Life goes on; if you are in a church like mine, everyone likes to hug you when they see you. It often happens quickly and without warning. If you pull away from them because you fear the pain, it will appear as if you do not want their hug. It can be a challenging option to prevent the hug or deal with the pain. I learned this the hard way from seeing the reaction of the first person that hugged me after those cracked ribs. I stepped back in pain and was quite animated, and I still cannot imagine her first thoughts. It took at least a minute to explain and tell the story.

That was all it took for me to realize that pain was not the opposite of love. This person unconditionally loved me as a fellow human being, and my pain would not stop that sense of love. I decided that I would not let my pain get in the way of hugs. Hugs had become too precious for me to lose. Somehow, over the weeks it took for my ribcage to get better, I convinced myself not to show the pain. Sometimes the pain levels pre-registered in my brain as minor to non-existent in reverence to the unconditional love that went with them. Effectively with mind over matter, I figured out how to cope with pain without showing or expressing my internal anguish to people.

As I have gotten older over the years, with changing weather or hard work, my body tells me all the dozens of places I have done bone damage. On top of that, I have underlying conditions that have been irritated because of car accidents. In all honesty, not a day goes by that pain is not present. I am not trying to complain. Instead, I acknowledge that aging brings a been there, done that appreciation and quiet understanding that I know in you.

You already know that the love surrounding you is not the opposite of pain. You would never feel love if pain was in the way of stopping the ability for you to receive love. Likewise if pain stopped you from loving someone then you would always be alone in your pain. People around you may perceive they were being pushed away because it could seem like you are not interested. You also know that pain is not only physical but emotional and spiritual, too. For instance, you may have lost a dear friend.

Being older, you may have lost both parents or even a child. There is deep emotional pain in these situations, and I know you have learned how to receive freely given love from others during these times. When I first noticed this phenomenon, it was remarkable how grieving then healing can occur faster and with joy. It is self-evident that we can learn to recognize that letting our pain show in anger, despair, and intolerance to others will block love from flowing inward or outward. Until Jesus' last breath, He did not let His pain, suffering, and despair get in the way of His love:

> Jesus cried out in a loud voice, "Father, into your hands I commend my spirit"; and when he had said this he breathed his last (Luke 23:46).

We can learn to reject these negative feelings that come with all types of pain. By substituting and remembering when we have received unconditional love, we can appreciate that pain is not the opposite of love.

PRACTICE *NOT EXPECTING ANYTHING* MAKES US PERFECT

When my wife and I started to get serious about our relationship, she introduced me to her family. From that point on, I was welcomed to her family's gatherings. I joyfully remember her seven siblings' birthdays, celebrations, and holidays. My favorite was the Easter egg hunt. My wife's father would spend many hours putting out hundreds of eggs for the children of the forty-plus people gathered. As he started getting older, it became harder to keep going with all these functions. All seven siblings volunteered to take over these events. Without even hesitating, my wife and I said we would take Easter.

I did not blindly go into this experience because I had admired and told her father each time I appreciated how much work he put into the Easter hunt. The first year I managed it at our yard, I realized I had underestimated the amount of work involved, and I was exhausted after an entire day spent hiding the hundreds of eggs. I knew the following year I needed to take a different approach. In the end, it was an attitude change. My solution was quite simple: as I planted each egg in its unique location, I would think of the person who would find it and my joy with them. I ended the day planting each egg with more energy than I had started.

As the years went by, I expected these hunts to pass on to their children because the current generation was getting well past an average age to find the eggs. However, that has not happened. I am now putting out eggs for twenty- and thirty-year-old adults to find. I realized that to keep doing it, I had to change the format of the Easter egg experience. I now use a scavenger clue-based format, changing the game each year. It is remarkable how this Easter experience has kept all these adult children committed to gathering each year.

The effort to put this newer format together has dramatically increased the process' time. I have to start thinking and planning what I will surprise the adult children with at least two months before Easter. It usually takes one to two evenings per clue to execute. Since there are so many adult children, I divide the game into four groups, each with a separate colored egg for clues they will use to find their unique dozen eggs. These games mean I need to create 48 clues.

I must also put these 48 clues into my yard the day before Easter. While this may seem like a lot of work, I have instead ignored all those distractive feelings and concentrated on the joy of seeing these adults genuinely enjoy themselves, laughing, and having a blast. I get many thanks each year from them, and I gratefully and humbly let them know I appreciate them. I love the smiles on their faces beaming when I continue to tell them how much joy I get from watching them turn into little children, even if just for an hour or so.

You are reading this when the Coronavirus is mostly behind us. In 2020 through 2022, I could not put this Easter experience together, and I deeply miss the opportunity to do so. In these joyful Easter experiences, I have entirely accepted that sometimes by ensuring we have no expectations, we can begin to appreciate what it means to become fully human with unconditional love. St. Paul gives us a peek at this perfection:

> [8] Love never fails. If there are prophecies, they will be brought to nothing; if tongues, they will cease; if knowledge, it will be brought to nothing. [9] For we know partially and we prophesy partially, [10] but when the perfect comes, the partial will pass away. [11] When I was a child, I used to talk as a child, think as a child, reason as a child; when I became a man, I put aside childish things. [12] At present

we see indistinctly, as in a mirror, but then face to face. At present I know partially; then I shall know fully, as I am fully known. [13] So faith, hope, love remain, these three; but the greatest of these is love (1 Corinthians 13:8-13).

The idea of practicing not having expectations, especially with our love, is challenging. However, giving ourselves to these moments in our lives can lead to the possibility of desiring to become perfect. Wouldn't it be wonderful if all organizations had this humbling goal in mind?

CHEERFULNESS

IMPROVING OURSELVES

I have been in the software industry now for almost 50 years. The old way to build software was to have a single static code set with everything that needed to be included. Sometimes if you were good at coding, you could create switches that you could use to shut off the features you had made, which visually reduced the clutter. When I started my own company over twenty-five years ago, we had to use this type of coding because that was the only technique available.

There was a massive shift in coding for a few years, so we decided to start over, moving to a more modular approach familiar to you as plastic building blocks. Our software became renewed around this metaphor of an old childhood toy to give our customers even more flexibility. Five years ago, I moved to an even more fine-grain (tiny building blocks), agile (flexible and quick) approach. The benefit is that the software is less expensive as the customer only needs to purchase the necessary functionality. In addition, deploying the software and the incremental changes customers may need over time became more manageable.

The need to stay current with my company's software forms a personal analogy. Two decades ago, I started to have a solid need to rebuild myself into a better man. When I examined the task, I knew that having a St. Paul-type instant conversion experience was not likely. Possibly because of my stubbornness, I can only change little by little, exchanging my approach to life here and there as I identified each area that needed work. I did not foresee that the tools to do so were readily available. It takes significant patience and *do-overs* to swap out the bad with the good from personal experience. The hardest part of *improving myself* has been not disclosing my desired individual changes or details. In all honesty, it is a brutal and mentally painful process as I analyze my way out, but all the while, I am attempting to be cheerful.

There have been significant setbacks, attempts that result in failures, and often a lot of effort, even for minimal changes. I have a long way to go, which will take well beyond my lifetime at the current rate, but in the meantime, I can already sense the positive actions of the replacement parts. For instance, one significant change I made was to dedicate a much larger percentage of my time to prayer. I am an early riser, so I wake up in a quiet house. I take advantage of that time to meditate, reflect, and thank God for the peace this quiet time provides. Without it, I am confident that the rough times in my business and personal life would have many sharp edges. I have recognized that these sharp edges are where damage can occur. My anger shows more, my patience grows thin, I forget to thank others, and I lose my capacity to be cheerful.

We are all unique in our ways, with both *good* and *needs improvement* attributes. If each of us looked inside, we may find something we can immediately recognize that would make us better men. Perhaps you think you are already in pretty decent shape. If you asked your significant other or best friend to suggest improvements, I suspect they can suggest a change. You will have to assure them you will take anything they say a constructive criticism and stick to it.

You may even think there is no apparent advantage to the work required to improve yourself. We are in a constant state of learning worldly things. As an example, I am old enough to remember that to communicate using the internet I had to put rubber cups over the ends of phone headset. At that time the early internet was so slow I would have to wait before typing the next character. Now I can watch high resolution movies using the internet. I had to work very hard adapting to many internet changes over the last five decades. Without doing so I could not own a small software company focused on making knowledge accessible.

We are spiritual people. Our spiritual capacity can always increase; shouldn't we put the same energy into that part of our lives. Our spiritual capital is the inner driver we display to the world through positive emotions. Doing so requires hard work and exercise no matter what part of our self it is applied to. The world needs to see us exercising this outward expression of the result of what happens when we work at improving ourselves to best utilize our gifts. Otherwise, those that are not cheerful could not learn how to be full of joy and cheer. St Paul gives us the courage to do so:

> [6] Since we have gifts that differ according to the grace given to us, let us exercise them: if prophecy, in proportion to the faith; [7] if ministry, in ministering; if one is a teacher, in teaching; [8] if one exhorts, in exhortation; if one contributes, in generosity; if one is

over others, with diligence; if one does acts of mercy, with cheerfulness (Romans 12:6-8).

It does not matter how your cheerfulness shows up. Mine is noticeable in my humor. For example, I have to be very careful because I have never been able to tell a joke, so I have a dry sense of humor. I can now make light of myself and take ribbing, smiling, and laughing at my quirks. I have become more vulnerable in conversation, which allows the other person to see behind the curtain. Occasionally the person sees it is safe for them to do the same. When this happens, my cheerfulness shows in my words and body language. I now know the truth and the possible depths of friendship when this kind of trust develops.

I would challenge you to ask yourself, "Am I a cheerful person internally?" You could consciously think about how cheerful you are during one entire day. If you believe you are a cheerful person to others, that is fantastic because people in our relationships need to cheer up. If not, find your style and rhythm to get to where you believe you are cheerful. Take it from someone who finally perceived I used to be cheerful but lost my way. With a lot of work over a couple of decades, I am becoming cheerful again, despite everything around me that seems to take the desire away. It is scary to allow change to reshape who we are, but don't you like being around cheerful people, so shouldn't you be one of them?

HAVING TO DO WHAT YOU
DO NOT WANT TO DO

We have all had the situation of doing something we do not want. Our reactions range from "oh, all right, I will do it" to "no way am I going to do this," but we often cave in and do it. These situations can involve a simple task where you are the only one involved to one or more people involved. If another person initiates the request, there are often residual or human emotions that you might feel, such as the other person owes you something in return or outright resentment. In some cases, we hold on to a longer-term grudge against

153

the person that can grow negatively stronger if there are additional requests.

The internal emotional turmoil from having to do something we do not want to do can be destructive. Let's turn this around to the other side of the coin. There are also things you like to do that are pretty enjoyable. Many make you quite cheerful, and you clearly show it in your disposition and facial expressions. Some of these are personal such as being outside or fully present with someone you love. You all volunteer to help out others without any conditions or expectations. When you do so, you feel you are doing something that will bring dignity and raise that person.

So what is the difference between those things you want to do and those that bring you cheerfulness? I have concluded that I can't pick and choose which of these came from God in my life. I have also concluded that I cannot predict which things will have a ripple effect in the universe surrounding my life. I have figured out that my attitude gets in the way of perceiving the benefit of the outcome. So the real difference is that I know the benefit from one side of the coin since I am in control. In the more negative or opposite case, since I do not want to do it, I will ignore the fact there could be a benefit.

When taken in this light, those things I do not want to do, have no internal motivation and cause me to be more selfish to diminish the outcome. Ouch, this is not who I want to be, nor should you wish to be this full of doubt and negative feelings. How can we give on one hand only when we want to? What happens when we do not consider the *knock on the door* might be Jesus in the book of Revelation?

> *Behold, I stand at the door and knock. If anyone hears my voice and opens the door, [then] I will enter his house and dine with him, and he with me* (Revelation 3:20).

What if that unknown knock might have ramifications that we do not yet understand?

So how can we take the side of the coin we do not like to let it yield an output like the side of the coin we do like? From deeply personal experience, I can tell you it is not easy, and if you choose to try to do so, it does not happen overnight. In my case, it has been a decade for me to begin the concept and have it work more naturally. I have reached an equilibrium since working on this correction in my life. Now I find more times than not, that I like the side of the coin, whether it is something I want to do or not.

It comes down to one often tough decision. Do I believe that what I am being asked to do could have been destined for me to do? One trick I have done to help decide is to take a long breath when asked. I don't know about you, but my reaction to anything that appears on my face in different intensities is based on how I instantly feel about it. My children knew this at a very early age. I remember my youngest daughter letting me know as a teenager that I had a tell. For example, I know it is relatively easy to tell when I lying. A range of changes starts with my ears turning various shaded of red, and next my face does the same. Lastly, for a more significant attempt at a lie, my eyebrow twitches. Obviously, I am a lousy poker player.

Everyone has their tell, and as people become familiar with us, they begin to read us. If you have a spouse, trust me, they know your tells. By taking a single conscience breath, you can slow down this tell from appearing for a fraction of a second and give your brain a chance to process what you have just been asked to do. If you do this, you can minimize your tell. Since people are used to processing ranges of tells, they often ignore the small tells. This fraction of a second to get to a minimized tell allows you to be more composed with your response.

It is this composure that then allows you the opportunity to decide to do the task because you think it might be destined or not. If it is ordained, then you have to work on doing it cheerfully. Even if this technique only works occasionally, you are cheerful, at least during those times. A positive change in anything we try is an acknowledgment that we have been successful with the transaction. You all can choose cheerfulness or appear burdened.

Think of it this way. I suspect you would rather all hang around with a cheerful person. Wouldn't you want this from those with whom you are associated? If so, it is a two-way street; you must practice it to get it right.

WEARING A SMILE

Despite their situation, we all know people that seem to wear a smile all the time. You may not see it in the upward curve of their lips but in their disposition, posture, the brightness in their eyes, and the desire to be present and available for others. To be honest, I struggle with trying to be that kind of person. As someone who has had constant neck pain for decades, it is hard to physically show a smile. However, I hope that people see it in different ways

Many years ago, after one of our meetings, I saw one of our members sitting at a table writing notes. He noticed me approaching him and immediately turned his full attention to me. We had known each other for years but never had a deep one-on-one conversation. What drew me to reach out to him was for the first time he was on the list of people our members were asked to keep in our thoughts and prayers.

I wasn't oblivious to his situation; I knew that he had that particular way of walking for years, so I knew he had hip or leg problems. That evening, since he was alone, I thought asking why we might be praying for him was ok. I can relate to suffering and the attempt to keep it far enough out of the way to allow a different focus. At that moment with him, if nothing else, I wanted him to know very personally how much I appreciated everything he had done. I intended to bring a little cheerfulness into view for him.

After briefly acknowledging my thoughts and gratitude, he downplayed what was happening for him and flipped the subject to how I was doing. I felt safe and comfortable sharing some details with him, and all of a sudden, it was like playing a ping-pong game. We moved outside of the original thought, jumping from topic to topic, realizing a tremendous amount of common ground. We were wearing our smiles in various ways as we kept going on our own been there and done that situations. I do not remember any of the conversation details because what became important to me was his grace in the encounter.

His empathetic nature of being positive and giving and consuming 100% of himself for us created a strong foundation for years to come with us. In less than fifteen minutes, I renewed my desire to be more present to others. I challenged myself to have an outward smile. Because of that one conversation, I began working on improving my emphatic desire again.

More than a decade after this conversation with him, he passed on to his next life in Heaven. In all that time, I never saw him show anything other than a smile that glowed from within him. Whenever I looked at him in all those years, I knew he was suffering. Like him, I am also gradually transitioning to putting aside the things inside that no longer need to get in the way of being positive.

When I learned he had passed, I instantly asked our priest if I could serve as a Eucharistic Minister at his funeral. I wanted to honor him in the best way I knew. Participating as a server in the Communion ritual as a member of the body of Christians was a good way for me to do so. Since I had previously confided with the priest about my own struggles, I think he understood why I asked. As each person walked up to receive, I did not hide my glazed-over eyes, and I made sure each person could see my smile inside. I wanted them to see that our friend loved God and neighbor and was now gloried with Christ.

28 We know that all things work for good for those who love God, who are called according to his purpose. 29 For those he foreknew he also predestined to be conformed to the image of his Son, so that he might be the firstborn among many brothers. 30 And those he predestined he also called; and those he

called he also justified; and those he justified he also glorified (Romans 8:28-30).

This story does not end here because I expressed gratitude with a story from my early religious education memories in our next KoC monthly meeting. I remember telling my religious education teacher I had just lost an aunt to kidney disease. She said that every time I thought of my aunt, a beautiful way to acknowledge that thought would be to smile and say, "Hi, Auntie." I have never ceased doing that for all the people that come to mind over the years. All those present at our KoC meeting heard me proclaim that I am blessed to be able to say, Hi, Tony!

HAPPINESS

OUR PLANS

I fell in love with my wife as a very young man, and despite our young age, we decided to get married. One of my quirks is that I did not want to have children right away for various reasons. All of them (looking back) I would call selfish today. One of the primary reasons was that I had convinced myself I was overwhelmed with the unknown because I did not have an excellent example to fall back on in my youth. I promised my wife that I would be ready at 30, and true to my word, our daughter was born then. God must have poured on the grace as I found myself loving her and my other two children beyond words. That led to me getting involved in their scouts, sports, and religious education because I liked sharing what I knew about life. I had started to learn to trust my faith. My son and I love the outdoors, so scouting was a natural choice.

I thought things were going along ok, believing I could control my path in life. However, various hiccups in my plans turned my life upside down. I had started my own company, going along at multiple times of over 100% year-to-year growth. Then the evil events of 911 changed all of our lives. I came close to losing my company, almost joining the ranks of many other failed businesses. Describing the turmoil plaguing me during the recovery period after 911 is difficult and painful because every plan I made was crushed.

Then my life took a significant turn during a hike deep in the forest. I suddenly realized I could not control my plans, no matter what I previously believed. Among other things that brought me to what should have been obvious was that I was running a company that went from exciting to dreadful. I could tell that something else was brewing outside of my control, and I had to let it in. It took another long hike in the forest to let the epiphany occur.

All alone, I understood that I had been given the desire to help others in a spiritual context. I instantly knew that I needed to write down my thoughts and meditations. I started shifting my mindset from the struggle of running a business to thinking about what was required to do so. My plans to become a multi-millionaire with my business dissipated. Being a strategic thinker of big plans turned to how I could help others one at a time. A strange turn of events made me understand that I should return to college when I was 50 years old. At 55, I received another graduate degree. This one was in pastoral ministry. My teenage thoughts of possibly being a celebate focused on religion had manifested into a slightly different reality.

In my wildest dreams, I could never predict the person I have become. God has taken me on an incredible journey of priority to seek first the kingdom of God and his righteousness, and all these things will be given you (Matthew 6:33). I look back and wonder about situations where I have resisted what may have been a better path. Perhaps I am maturing or want to have that childlike innocence again because I consider options more freely. I have learned that I cannot see hidden values and abilities without opening my heart to possibilities. I am still surprised when something happens, and I ignore my everyday logical thinking about all the options to address them and instead trust my gut. The last decade has been filled with the realization that goals provide motivation, but plans need constant updating because they are highly subject to change.

The sense of the future does not mean we should not have goals, but rather, their rigidity needs to be far more flexible. The reality of being people of honor, integrity, righteousness, and compassion means the goal we want to happen become more focused on the day-to-day.

DISCOVERING THE LITTLE THINGS

I know you all have parts of your life that must make you very happy. Some are easily recognized, such as when your spouse is satisfied, so are you. Or how about when you see children laughing and playing? Doesn't that bring a smile to your face? If you have children, grandchildren, or children you care for, you can appreciate the excitement of anything new unfolding. When they do something that brings them to wonder and talk about it with you, don't you immerse yourself in that same wonder?

Those little things are also harder to detect and define as happiness. Since I have hearing loss and am musically tone-deaf, I find myself giving my meanings to song lyrics. I admit that I know how I think about the lyrics is probably not what the artist intended. My faith sometimes causes me to see positive connections with spiritual values. When I discover songs that speak and move me, I feel a subtle but essential type of happiness. Happiness often relates to our nature as humans, often as non-verbal communication. My favorite lyrics tug at my heart when they represent who I am or what to be or do.

An example is a song by Damien Rice titled "Cold Water." The lyrics are haunting and draw out pictures in my mind of the need to help others. I imagine someone in trouble with their hand reaching out, and I have been guided toward them by the Lord in the hope that I can help. The desire has happened dozens of times, and I have also been on the receiving end. While what I may have for the other might be small, I feel immense joy and happiness because I have responded to the call.

Here is a stanza from *Cold Water* by Damien Rice[6] that touches a nerve whenever I hear it.

Cold, cold water surrounds me now
And all I've got is your hand (surrounds me now)
Lord (can you hear me?)
Lord (can you hear me now?)
Lord (can you hear me?)
Aah, lost, am I lost without you?

When I have unconditionally helped someone, even subtly, I get the happiness of sharing something from deep within myself. There is no ego or pride, no need to talk about what I have done, and no need to expect anything, just a sense that I have done the right thing at that moment. These small moments add up over time living in a subtle repository in my mind. Sometimes, I have to think about something that happened even years ago to bring on a burst of happiness.

You may have a different way of knowing these moments, finding inspiration, and hearing your song expressed by someone else without them even knowing you. These threads of being connected to someone else, an organization, or a shared community are the little things we can recall that work like adrenaline. Each time we do, the memory of that happiness helps us drive forward towards doing it again in whatever way we are called to do it. Paul offered a prayer to the Ephesians (and to you) regarding how we can continue to gladden our hearts:

> [15] Therefore, I, too, hearing of your faith in the Lord Jesus and of your love for all the holy ones, [16] do not cease giving thanks for you, remembering you in my prayers, [17] that the God of our Lord Jesus Christ, the Father of glory, may give you a spirit of wisdom and revelation resulting in knowledge of him. [18] May the eyes of [your] hearts be enlightened, that you may know what is the hope that belongs to his call, what are the riches of glory in his

inheritance among the holy ones (Ephesians 1:15-18).

I suggest you take the time to reflect on the wonder and awe of these little things. I would be willing to bet that some of them bring you orders of magnitude more happiness than the effort that went into them.

BEYOND SATISFIED WITH DECISIONS
ALL THE WAY TO HAPPY

As a small software company owner, I have had to make tough business decisions that can tear the fabric of my standards of morality. Years ago, I had a complex dilemma because we had a legally contracted partner in Europe selling our software who was not being honest. They kept the money from selling our software and support services and did not tell us. We found out the hard way because they went out of business, and their customers started calling us directly for the support they were supposed to get. Since we had no record or income from the devious partner, we had no choice but to provide support or get a bad name in the industry. We lost over $250,000 from this deal gone wrong.

We could not quickly find another partner we could trust. Many of these European customers left us because U.S.-based companies must have a European-based representative. Just before I decided that I was going to call my company's business attorney, I called a Christian friend who was a generalized attorney. For a personal favor, I asked for his suggestion of what he could do. I was shocked when he felt there was nothing I could do. I would have to spend more than I had lost to recover even a tiny fraction of what it would cost to pursue it. He said I had very little chance at success without European legal representation. He pointed out how difficult it would be to find a trusted attorney in Europe.

My desire for vengeance could not be realized due to the time and money it would take to pursue the vengeance. If I had made that choice out of spite, I would have had an additional financial loss, I would have been drawn away from running my company, and most likely have put excessive stress on my employees and family. As it is, I almost went out of business because of this situation. I had unwittingly been forced into pure unadulterated evil and was devasted. As the company owner, it was my fault for not seeing through the façade of this supposed partner who had signed contracts with us. In truth, it was starting to take a toll on my health and well-being.

I had to make the most challenging choice of my business career: either continue to feel the way I did or accept the reality of the situation and move on. Among the elements at play was that I had incorrectly started to suspect even our best U.S. reseller partners, thinking they could do the same at any moment. I had also barely survived as a business after 9/11 because many of our partners had gone out of business themselves. In effect, this disaster was affecting my relationships with almost everyone. My prayer life also suffered because I thought the solution was to spend all my time saving my company over everything else. It was a very dark period for me.

One evening before bedtime, I gave up and told God I needed help. The following day, I realized I had accepted the situation and needed to return to my old self quickly. It wasn't a sense of recharge or anything like that but a subtle reminder that I could turn the situation around. Over the next few weeks, I knew I had to effectively put everything that happened into the trash can to be thrown away.

More importantly, I had to be satisfied with that decision and not turn back from it. It took almost two years to return to where I was, but I did. Over time I have grown to be happy with the decision because it proved my worth was more than just money; it was a sense of testing my morality. What this ruthless organization did was ethically wrong. However, the amount of energy I would have used to recover a small portion of what was stolen was overwhelming. If I had done so, I suspect my time and attention to others would have been reduced, potentially changing my personal relationships. Jesus teaching me about retaliation kept coming to mind throughout the entire ordeal:

> "You have heard that it was said, 'An eye for an eye and a tooth for a tooth.' But I say to you, offer no resistance to one who is evil (Matthew 5:38-39a).

I now know with 100% certainty that I made the right decision. While it took time, my faith in others has been fully restored.

Something quite remarkable happened to me because of this situation. I now put the morality question front and center. I no longer react to these types of problems with any sense of getting even or fighting back. I have discovered that happiness is within reach, even in the worst of any situation. We have to find and hold onto the strand of hope of happiness, no matter how small it might initially feel.

I have grown accustomed to telling this story to other business owners and anyone struggling with a tough decision. I end my story with the choice to be happy, and sometimes we may have to manufacture it from the thinnest of strands. I believe we all have the inner capacity to dig deep and make it happen.

GRATITUDE

LEAVENING

While I was pursuing my Pastoral Ministry degree, one of the courses was *Spiritual and Faith Formation*. We were discussing the metaphor of being leavening agents. You may recall that un-leavened bread is flat. As the yeast consumes the sugars, yeast expels gas into inescapable air pockets, causing the bread to be leavened. This process adds volume to the flour, and in a short time, the bread rises and grows.

Providentially, that same week my son made yogurt from scratch. The process of making yogurt is similar, except a small amount of existing yogurt replaces the yeast. The steps to do so is relatively easy. You gently warm a gallon of milk to prepare it for the culture. Then you mix in one spoonful of ordinary yogurt (culture) to the milk, refrigerate it, and in as little as 24 hours later, that gallon of milk is well on its way to becoming yogurt.

I remember the evening that I had a little story prepared for the end of our Knight's meeting. Just before the start of the meeting, my mind started to go in a different direction. The thought hit me that this is what true Knights are to the world around us. I had to save the story I had planned and instead told the men how vital our behavior, work, and actions are. Outside of the meeting, we are also members of something greater. We have our families and jobs where we interact with other people. We have many hobbies where we encounter people. We have close friends with whom we sometimes share very personal discussions. In these moments when we are together, most often, our relationships become incrementally stronger.

What happens after each of these times we are with each other? What kinds of impressions have we left with them? Have we been that small spoonful of yogurt filled with hope, good thoughts, and change agents for positive direction? We can make meaningful differences in people's lives, even for those we do not know, by trusting our small humble actions. If we are authentic by being who we are, we leave a subtle imprint on them, even if it lies dormant deep inside their consciousness.

It does not take much analysis to see that I have been *raised* by whatever good has happened regarding others during our meetings. This goodness in the meeting has found a home within me and continues to grow if I allow it. I have had the opportunity to become leavened. I know this is true because my wife will smile when I go home after the meetings. She knows I will come home happy. That moment has been repeated hundreds of times, and I can personally attest to its power. For the rest of the evening, my wife and I smile as I share my joy. That tells me that some leavening has occurred. Through this process, I have become an example of Jesus's woman using the yeast parable. He spoke to them in another parable.

> The kingdom of heaven is like yeast that a woman took and mixed with three measures of wheat flour until the whole batch was leavened (Matthew 13:33).

I have learned to be more open to others in my willingness to share my own life lessons.

Without realizing it, these little sparks of goodness continue into the next day. It is remarkable how I have learned that I can be that yeast or that spoonful of yogurt. I have become responsible for sharing who I am with others. That responsibility had gone from an unconscious feeling in the early days of when I first joined our organization to now full-blown recognition.

Like the rest of you, I am sure the sense of what I gathered during the meeting dissipates. Honestly, I am trying to figure out how to make it last longer. I know I have made forward progress because every so often, I realize it is a few days later, and I still have that feeling. Perhaps you know this already, but I hope I have given you something to consider if you do not.

APPRECIATING THE WORK OF OTHERS

Several years ago, our church became the only Catholic church in our town due to the need by the diocese to consolidate. Many essential and beautiful items were saved to add or replace similar items within our building before the other Catholic church was sold. For instance, this included a hand-crafted wooden precious oil cabinet, a stunning tabernacle, and a wonderfully sculpted statue of Mary. For me, one of the most treasured and stunning items was a three-dimensional work of art collection of the Stations of the Cross.

Our pastor immediately appreciated their spiritual value and replaced the ones we had. The other church's parishioners must have worked physically and financially hard to have such beautiful works of art. The gift of awe and wonder must have been present in the parishioners to be moved and appreciative of the idea of enhancing their church. Art like this allows us to see the God-given gift of skills to each artist.

If we appreciate the gift from God to the religious artist, the phenomenon could also be considered a preview of what is to become. I have come to believe that many artists are trying to express goodness beyond themselves. For me, seeing what art represents is a glimpse of the unexpected. For example, years ago, we had a small group walk together to reflect on the Stations of the Cross each Friday during Lent. The Stations are artist renditions such as paintings or sculptures of the scenes of the *Passion of Christ*, which are the last few days of Jesus. Our newer art of the *Stations* are mounted along the inside perimeter walls between the window that looks out on the church's property. One side of the church building faces the parking lot.

I am always enthralled at the Twelfth Station, which is the scene of the moment Jesus died included in the Gospel of John: *When Jesus had taken the wine, he said, "It is finished." And bowing his head, he handed over the spirit (John 19:30).* This may seem like I am not respecting this moment of Jesus on the Cross when walking and praying the stations. I am joyful because I can look directly across the parking lot to our Food Truck in action with rows of cars buying fish and chips from that window.

As Christians as one in Christ's body, I see Christ's hands and feet at work outside in our parking lot. In a single glance at the art of the instant death of Christ, I also witness the risen Christ alive in a group of men and women volunteering for the Friday fish fries from that window. These people are metaphorically reenacting the multiplication of bread and fish Gospel story. One hundred percent of these fish fry profits go to various non-profit organizations that serve our community, such as the food pantry in town.

My net result is the impact of volunteers worldwide feeding Jesus' flock and behaving just as He would. I like to imagine what would happen if everyone acted as people unconditionally helping others. This realization was reinforced in a single view of the 12th Station, which I saw in the mingling of the action on the Cross and the Cross in action.

These people are all doing and being present for others to help the local community. In my walk of the stations, I realized I was also part of this group of people because I was in a spiritual world of prayer doing the same thing. At that moment, I was incredibly grateful to pray inside the church without them knowing. I captured the thought of knowing there was something more at play. When I finished the Stations, I sat in a pew row to reflect and understand. I concluded I had another perfect story *for the Good of the Order.* I have shared this story hundreds of times since that first realization.

To the right audience, be it one or many, it is still an extremely emotional few minutes when I tell the story. I had found a way to repeatedly express my full appreciation of gifts from God for the dedication of the people volunteering at the fish fry. That experience also reinforced how important it was to me to thank people when I see them doing unconditional things for others.

Conceptually the same as the people at the fish fry, volunteers worldwide are working hand in hand to make the world a better place silently and humbly. Each one will tell you they do so unconditionally without expecting a thank you. However, when you thank them, you also raise your hands in grateful joy to God. I would encourage you to consider increasing how often you gracefully acknowledge those who do good for your community. From my experiences, there is a significant return to me in the quiet thanks for my thanking them. The combination of recognizing and appreciating their sacrifice warms my heart because of Christ's sacrifice.

CAMPING FUN

My family and my wife's sister's family went camping together over the summer and had a great time. Saturday became interesting because six young adults camped in three small tents beside us. Earlier in the day, the three men and three women were having fun. That changed when evening came along, and the alcohol started flowing. Late that night, it became clear that the sleeping arrangements had not been previously considered. Two of them sorted it out right away and went into a tent.

The discussions began to include more *intensifiers* in each sentence with the other four. Our kids were sleeping, but these young adult voices started to get louder. I was about to step into this dilemma with my desire to quiet them down when one young woman settled the situation. Her words made it clear that he was not the man she preferred, yet in a few moments later, they walked hand in hand toward their tent.

I couldn't help sharing this story at our monthly meeting as this group of young adults seemed to consider what they did as expected behavior. It made me wonder about where the concept of other regular activities was headed. We are meant to be together, so I make every attempt possible not to judge. However, for me, the perfection of togetherness is a loving, tender relationship, not settling for whatever happened at the campsite.

I'll take a positive view of this experience and say that we can build on our virtues when we control ourselves (sometimes with help from various sources). With our strong belief in charity as a part of love, we must stand up and show our moral courage and fiber.

But wait, there is more reasoning to the story. I had gone camping in the near-exact same situation in my late teens, but we did not even consider breaking up into couples to sleep together. At the end of the evening, we each went innocently into our tents without any apparent carnal desires.

Interestingly, when I sometimes think about these different but otherwise same situations, I wonder if I was the one who had done something backward. Is it possible that I missed out on something? Each time, the result of my thoughts is that I am grateful that I did not think I was supposed to pair up. In that way, even in my youth, my instincts were to think of how the other person would feel. I could not see how I might push myself to want to make another person feel obligated somehow.

I am drawn to people and organizations that support my natural positive values of respecting and helping others. If I look around society today, there appears to be an increasing amount of self-centeredness and the desire and immediacy of correcting and satisfying wrongs. I am often not sure there is enough thought into the balance and considerations for an immediate effect. Undoubtedly, many of these wrongs are moral violations of what they should have been. However, I seriously question if getting to the right solution will adequately be addressed, so both sides are grateful for the result.

I cannot appreciate how these intense situations could feel resolved without the benefit of gratitude for both parties. One party may feel like the young adult who reluctantly settled for the other person while camping. I am all for expressing who we are as humans as long we consider the pros and cons and have gratitude.

I know from the experience of privately talking to someone at the receiving end of getting aid. She was grateful and humbled by what a charity-based fraternal group did for her. This dual-sided respect and gratitude are two of the most significant achievements we can accomplish toward becoming fully human. Paul discussed generosity with the Corinthians:

¹¹ You are being enriched in every way
for all generosity, which through us
produces thanksgiving to God, ¹² for the
administration of this public service is
not only supplying the needs of the holy
ones but is also overflowing in many
acts of thanksgiving to God
(2 Corinthians 9:11-12).

When there is gratitude, there is a
positive and lasting effect. I firmly believe that
actions that are not forced, coerced, or
demanded but done instead with silence and
knowing gratitude are what God would want.

HOPE

ENCOURAGING YOUTH TO SHARE
THE GIFT OF THEMSELVES

I have worked with youth and teens in a leadership capacity for over three decades. My experience includes team sports, scouts, and religious education. I have always readily and freely shared whatever knowledge I have learned since my youth. Giving children and young adults hope in their future comes to the surface in most of my conversations. It may sound cliché, but typically this means giving them examples of goodness and fairly treating others if they expect the same. In general, this concept is something I frequently witness with other adults when they are with teens. As someone with this focus, it is wonderful to be pleasantly surprised when we see a teen reflecting on their learning.

In scouts, the highest achievements are Eagle and Gold projects that benefit a community. Watching what these teens can do independently in leading a project after years of being guided to this point is a fantastic experience. These teens are working on projects with the collective nature of help from other scouts. When they do so, they are actualizing the meaning of hope.

Some of you sometimes think back to pews filled at church services. It is hard to imagine that just a few decades ago, we had to add expansion wings at our church building to accommodate those who sometimes had to stand around the outside perimeter. Now on an average Sunday, we might see our pews two-thirds occupied. In the back of any Christian's mind is the thought that organized religion is in jeopardy of disappearing

As someone who helps lead youth and religious education groups, I have firsthand evidence of our community's youth who will bring us forward. For instance, an older teen led a decade of the Rosary at one of our retreats. I saw myself in him as he struggled and worked his way through it. This young man wanted to pray with and for others despite the world's confusion. These same groups of young people have done some fantastic service projects for our community, so it is clear that prayer is part of their focus.

I witnessed the positive energy in them as they weeded our community garden that grows produce for our town's food pantry. I saw teens helping out in our closest city's Urban Missionaries ministry. I witnessed them beautifying the church property by pruning a patch of blackberries that had gone wild. Our youth have spent time in Haiti at the elderly facility we sponsor. This list is just some of the service work they have done without any prodding.

After any service event, we meet with the teens. The discussion seems to flow on how natural it is to be generous of themselves to our communities, including those beyond our borders. Just as important, they see the logic of how being organized in their faith has allowed them to enjoy each other's company while they worked together. We have some fantastic young people who will preserve the past and embrace the future. They have become wise as written in Proverbs: *Whoever cares for the poor lends to the Lord, who will pay back the sum in full* (Proverbs 19:17). While the spirit of hope of these young people may not qualify to make the daily prime-time news, I believe they represent a far larger unpublished movement of the heart.

OUR FIRE WITHIN

Every year on Ash Wednesday, we are anointed with ashes on our foreheads to remind us of God speaking to Adam and Eve:

> By the sweat of your brow
>   you shall eat bread,
> Until you return to the ground,
>   from which you were taken;
> For you are dust,
>   and to dust you shall return
>   (Genesis 3:19).

During the living part of our life, before we are dust again, we get a chance to turn away from those things that prevent us from being the good people God intends us to be. We can progressively be made better by giving ourselves to others with our time, talents, and treasures. This includes physically helping others, being fully present to someone by listening and praying for others. One of the less well-known forms of prayer you may already use is to just be. An example of to be is to ask the Spirit in stillness and quiet to give the beautifully burning flames of the collected treasure in your heart to someone who needs it more than you do.

Ash Wednesday ashes are formed from what remains after the fire of burning palm leaves. Fire is a two-edged sword because it can be destructive if it becomes out of control. As a scout leader, I have seen scouts take burning sticks and nearly start a forest fire. If I had not stopped what they were doing, I could imagine the news headlines if it had happened.

My wife and I live a short distance from the city. Trees and bushes in our yard constantly shed branches that fall to the ground. We can burn the brush for a short period each year. I clean down to dirt a few feet around where I will burn the brush to prevent a runaway fire. The fire metaphor can apply to those negatives that burn unattended inside us, leaving us with regrets and even singe the edges of our relationships. You can imagine that these negatives would be better off if they were ash instead of fire.

I know personally of many things in my life that have smoldered negative feelings. As a person who has grown into thinking in moderation and unity, it is hard to deal with extremes of *us and them* situations. For example, I know firsthand how political oil can flame the fire inside me to escape its boundaries. For decades now, every morning when I get up, I try to think of things I can work on properly burning to be free of the burden they can put on me.

I spent much of my early adult life gathering things that would make me look successful. When I look back, these included nice cars, making my home more extensive and comfortable, and quality suits for work. I feel like I have been burning away that part of myself to reveal a more peaceful person who instead lets the fire within warm my heart. My ashes are experiences I have learned from but not entirely forgotten as reminders. You could probably see that difference if you had known me forty years ago. Controlling the fire inside is a delicate balance.

Ashes are a great way of thinking about the beginnings of this process. If we think about a controlled physical fire, such as in a fire pit or fireplace, a new fire is often created on top of ashes already there. Starting a new fire on top of existing ashes is quite common. You do not have to throw away those ashes because they can help contain the fire from spreading beyond where it should be. The ashes become a base for a fire that will turn out differently each time.

Ashes form a starting point reminding us that we can begin over each day in a controlled way that we watch over and maintain. I used a wood stove to heat my house years ago. I needed to keep that fire going so the house's temperature would make it livable. On frigid days, if I let it go out, it would take a while to warm the home, and it would be a lot more work. We need a fire that keeps us warm but does not burn us or someone else.

Our task throughout life is to maintain our fire well. Like me, your fire can move outside boundaries you do not desire. Yet, you have your own techniques to get it under control, sometimes starting over again on top of those ashes. Isn't it great to know that you build new fires on top of the learned ashes? We can join around our common fires and cheer each other on so that personal fires within glow and radiate outward in many signs of joy, compassion, and love.

LONG-TERM THINKING ABOUT OTHERS

Brotherhood and sisterhood as a concept are difficult to describe. With society moving more towards self rather than a giving group to others as the center, the reality of common concern and balanced unity seems to have less weight. How we use naming is also changing. I have to admit I have become selective, liking some of the name changes and pushing back on some, especially with the tongue twisters. I do not mind using personhood instead of brotherhood or sisterhood for some situations, as we can gather as a group of brothers and sisters, and we can also gather as a group of people.

I believe it is acceptable to have an opportunity to let our values adapt to a situation. There is a relatively new product I can use as a metaphor to describe this adaptability. If you do any packing and shipping or receiving of delicate items, you probably know of a packaging called *peanuts*. New environmentally friendly packing peanuts are now available for consideration.

These light green biodegradable packing peanuts almost entirely dissolve when exposed to moisture. When you placed one of the peanuts in a glass of water, you can see the proteins and starch break apart but still exist in a different form. The water gets cloudy and filled with microscopic partials from within the peanuts. As a metaphor, what started as a complete peanut in brotherhood or sisterhood is easily made into personhood without losing the original ingredients. The values instilled in the brotherhood (peanut in full shape), such as charity, are still present in personhood (distributed into the water *society*). The values of brotherhood or sisterhood are not lost but become immersed throughout.

Like the packing peanut, you can change your form as you are whole when bound in brotherhood or sisterhood or in any combined group serving others and whole with others in personhood. Your values and virtues are still intact and not watered down even when you are distributed into society. While pushing back on values directly focusing on the self has become more difficult, we should still try. We tend to go along with things when we sometimes need to use our distributed values. For example, are we entirely utilizing the strength of *group* to resist the tendencies in society to put down faith in God and its positive influence on organizations?

My particular brotherhood group confirms that because it is permanently stated in the charter and etched on my heart as a sense of unconditional love. We are supposed to love our neighbor, yet without an underlying sense of permission to do so freely, how do we show this love? For example, positive emotions are involved in how our organization clearly and routinely utilizes our talents and gifts to make our community a wholesome and better place to live.

I suspect many of you are like me. An immense sense of joy in what we do for others is hidden behind the scenes because we become humble. Perhaps this internal sense is all you need, but in my aging, I need not be vague but more outwardly to humbly show the light within to others. Maybe your internal light becomes visible without words, is contagious, and sustains you, giving meaning to your life. You may also feel like a cocoon that wants to open its wings into a butterfly to fly freely.

I am beginning to believe I have permission to put my feelings into words. At the moment, I am at the crawling stage of learning how to do so. It seems logical to take the time because I can walk towards emotional freedom once I can stand with others who want to go beyond their own self to share with others. In my family, work, and groups I belong to, I have a sense of knowing people who feel similar in their long-term thinking about helping others. I hope that everyone worldwide can enjoy this same sense of generosity. We all have the capacity for compassion, kindness, and love within our sisterhoods, brotherhoods, and beyond into our universal personhoods with words and actions. David in Psalm 133 speaks of this capacity:

> A song of ascents. Of David.
> How good and how pleasant it is,
>   when brothers dwell together as one!
> Like fine oil on the head,
>   running down upon the beard,
> Upon the beard of Aaron,
>   upon the collar of his robe.
> Like dew of Hermon coming down
>   upon the mountains of Zion.
> There the Lord has decreed a blessing,
>   life for evermore! (Psalm 133)

CLOSING THOUGHTS

I recently closed a meeting discussing the difficulty of handling a freshly caught eel. It is hard to contain the slippery all-muscle eel to get the hook out so you can let it return to the water. I brought up my multiple experiences of catching and releasing eels because I had been getting a series of blood tests. My veins do not want the needle to slip in because they are like those eels, so it usually takes many tries to get the blood flowing into the test tubes. I recently had a nurse who pushed down hard on a vein to get the needle in.

It reminded me of how I usually get that fishing hook out. I find a spot to put the eel on the ground and gently but firmly hold it in place long enough to remove the hook so the eel can return to the water. We all have been held in place because of COVID, unable to do our everyday routines. It is easy to see that this pandemic has pushed people to the edge and sometimes even over the edge. I believe the effect of this trapped feeling has caused twisting, turning, wiggling, and pushing society more than usual. One of the results is a dramatic increase in the elevation of causes that have left many of us bewildered. It feels like a magnifying glass is suddenly being used to identify all that is wrong.

I suggest remembering how many beautiful changes happened in our lifetimes in how we treat each other by accepting and appreciating the logic behind each one. We have entered a wave of history with compressed information and events than we have known before. Given that we are not used to this speed of change, we may have to allow ourselves to be gently *held* *down* to absorb and understand before we are let go. However, if our virtues are impacted, it is also appropriate to nudge back.

ENDNOTES

[1] For example, Henry M. Robert III, Daniel H Honemann, Thomas J Balch, Daniel E. Seabold, Shmuel Gerber. *Robert's Rules of Order*, 12th ed., New York: PublicAffairs, 2020.

[2] *Wiktionary* is a free dictionary under the Creative Commons Attribution-ShareAlike 3.0 Unported License and the GNU Free Documentation License.

[3] All Scripture in this book is used with permission from **New American Bible, revised edition** © 2010, 1991, 1986, 1970 Confraternity of Christian Doctrine, Inc., Washington, DC All Rights Reserved.

[4] Father Michael J. McGivney has just been recognized as a Blessed. A Blessed is a Catholic person that is formally recognized as someone, among other attributes, who has been heroically virtuous, offered their life for others, and is worthy of imitation. (United States Conference of Catholic Bishops - https://www.usccb.org/offices/public-affairs/saints).

[5] More information on James Tissot at the Brooklyn Museum: https://www.brooklynmuseum.org/exhibitions/james_tissot

[6] Damien Rice, *Cold Water*, **Album O**, 14th Floor, Warner Music (UK/Ireland), Vector (US), 2002. https://youtu.be/_rPeRkVmCtg.

ABOUT THE AUTHOR

Jerry is a happily married practicing Catholic living in Central Massachusetts (New England, USA). He is actively involved in a variety of both being and doing ministries. To be present to God and others by waiting is a difficult challenge, as it is his nature to react by finding solutions to every problem immediately. His attempts to do so would not be possible if he did not take time for prayer. His life experiences far outweigh his computer technology, graduate business, and pastoral ministry degrees. His observation is that his education in knowing the language of business, and personal beliefs, along with his doubting Thomas within, appropriately mingles the human and divine nature of who he is. He has found that he quickly burns out, attempting to fight every wrong he observes.

Jerry has realized that his specific commission means he must responsibly identify and use his God-given gifts. He tries to share his belief in the love of God and neighbor as appropriately as possible, especially knowing he has a choice in accepting God's will. Jerry loves writing about the ordinary times of God's peace, love, and actions. He firmly believes we can tap into an internal desire to know unconditional love.

Jerry appreciates and understands that what he writes can be radically different from the belief of others as he does lean on his experiences and background of practicing his faith. He firmly believes that whatever your faith might be can help shape you into someone willing to be kind and compassionate. He only asks that, as he would do with you, to regulate your reaction to his writings by accepting another person's belief that has the commonality for all that "God is love."

Please look for Jerry's other books on Amazon, Barnes & Noble, and other fine bookstores. They are also available through ShelteringTree.Earth website.

DISCUSSION GUIDE FOR SMALL GROUPS OR PERSONAL REFLECTION

1. Were there ideas in the collection of stories that prompted consideration of using positive emotions to close a meeting, and if so, why? Share your thoughts on a particular short story or emotion that resonated with your desire to have everyone memorably leave a gathering.

2. With a pre-announced premise that each vignette points to one or more emotions, can you describe to your group a triggering event that made sharing the stories possible? Share a life experience that stirs your creativity and cheerful nature. What are the reactions of the members of your group?

3. Can you align any of the short life experiences in the book as situations for you or someone you know in your group? Did you notice believability in the stories? If so, was there one that stood out and why?

Can you share one of your experiences that is hard to believe but true? Be sure to include the emotion that made the moment feel positive.

4. Learning to be vulnerable and sharing life transformations are challenging. Do you know people (including yourself) in your meetings who have the knack for exploring the positive values of various life experiences? Without embarrassing that person, ask them if they would be willing to share a life experience with your group at a future meeting.

5. A good joke teller can create a scene and outcome in a few sentences. At the other end of the spectrum is a full-length movie or an entire life. These various scene options can be memorable. Pick out a story in the book to read but leave out the last paragraph. Ask your group to predict the outcome or what you may have thought before the ending and share it with others. Read the conclusion and discuss how far off or close you were and why.

6. Read the last paragraph of one of the emotions. Share your own story that could resonate with the emotion. How did you want the members of your group to feel before the end of your story?

7. Everyone has their share of unclear resolutions in life. Using one of the stories, change the ending to your alternative ending. What did you sense from those present about speaking from the heart? Consider when you go to someone you trust or God to help with conflicts. Without *naming names*, bring up a current or lingering dispute among your group. How can you use what you have learned?

8. The vignettes in the book contain physical and spiritual settings ranging from personal, business, and cultural. Pick out a story where God had a significant role and one where God's influence was more subtle. What might be the reasons for that?

9. A few stories have an unresolved fluid settling of the heart, not a jointly agreed decision. Think about the times you have said we will have to agree that we disagree and yet left with a smile because you opened your heart to hear the other person. Can you share one without divulging confidences that ended friendly and was later re-opened for discussion?

10. I have good and bad days like you. I often wish it would have gone differently at the end of a difficult day. Some of the vignettes have unexpected twists and turns. Is there one that stands out in this regard? Is there a parallel to difficulty in some of your meetings? How could adding a *For the Good of the Order* impact a meeting that was tough to deal with?

11. I considered changing the title of For a Good of the Order to the first story title of *Everything Can be a Shiny Object*. Likewise, the painting on the cover does not seem to equate to the title. I faced the classic, which came first, the chicken or the

egg. After you have read a series of the stories, discuss whether the cover painting represents closing your meeting with something that evokes joy or other positive emotions.

12. I have read many beautiful books of different religions that agree on human virtues and morals. What ideas in the stories contain virtues or morals? Discuss how these values can influence your whole meeting, not just the ending.

13. Meetings sometimes seem like all work and business. Yet time after time, I am sure you recognize that the same people contributing can also encourage a movement of the heart. Did you notice that each story has aspects that lead to a similar reaction? Describe the characteristics someone would have to be able to use details and examples to highlight positive ideas for your group.

14. If you have faith beliefs, supporting what you say and do regarding your faith is natural. Undoubtably, the stories within are told from a Catholic perspective. How would you feel about adapting the general concepts in the book to your faith? I encourage you to do so. What would you change? Give an example.

15. There are 36 life experiences as short stories to consider. These experiences may lead you to a specific theme. What vignette drew you in and made you want to keep reading more stories and consideration of a *For the Good of the Order* for your group? Discuss how you could adapt variations of these stories or present your own stories or ideas for your group.

16. After reading the first story's title, you likely knew how an emotion would emerge from within other stories. Pick a story and describe how you saw the objective developing before the end. Can you see how you might do the same?

17. Pick out a vignette where you felt an internal resonance at a specific point in the story other than the ending. Resonance does not mean identical. However, in one of the stories, you may have had a moment that triggered a related memory or thought that brought back the joy in your life. If you are comfortable with it, share your story with the group. Have the group point out something that kept them waiting for the next thing you were going to say.

18. After reading one or two stories, it was probably obvious that the last paragraph would be a recommendation to those present. These stories took from 3-5 minutes to deliver at each meeting. How could you tell as you were reading you knew when the ending was coming? Discuss your thoughts about what you heard just before the closing paragraph. Can you consider doing the same for your group by telling a story that concludes with the lesson learned?

19. The last paragraph of each vignette was used for what the concept in the story could mean to the group. Many vignettes could have alternate or several thought-provoking *leave-behinds* for the endings. Discuss and justify a different closing with a new emotion.

20. These were personal stories with little need for proven or historical fact-checking. However, they are true stories that attempt, when possible, to leave out details. None of the stories are distorted or contrived. However, sometimes when we tell stories, details are necessary. Share your vignettes in two different ways. One has facts and data, and the other minimizes those details. Ask those present which method is best for your members and why.

21. Out of the 36 short stories, pick three of your favorites and discuss the choices you made. Examine the reasons you made. Could you see a natural progression of flow in the story? Was the primary message understandable? Did the technique and style

feel consistent? Compare your results with the others in your group. After working through these questions are you or someone in the group willing to try using *For the Good of the Order* in your meetings?

Our books will help you feed His sheep.

We are an exclusive publishing house. We specialize in
uplifting, inspirational, and positive adult, juvenile and
young adult, fiction and nonfiction, including poetry, native
histories and spiritual paths, sermons, lectio divina, and
pastoral and rabbinical resources in English, French, Spanish,
Indigenous languages, and tri- and bilingual versions.

Our readers, once they finish one of our books, will be able
to get up and face the world wiser, stronger, centered, and
with the assurance that we are not alone:
we are all a part of the Sheltering Tree on Earth.

If you as a writer feel that same calling, please refer to

ShelteringTree.Earth

www.ingramcontent.com/pod-product-compliance
Lightning Source LLC
Chambersburg PA
CBHW02082926060626
47169CB00003B/899